CRYPT of CTHULHU

Dedicated to the memory of Mable M. Price.

Published by Cryptic Publications.
Cover of *Crypt of Cthulhu* by Kate Reilly.
Drawings by Juan.

Crypt of Cthulhu

Issue # 114

St. John's Eve 2022

What was the Black Meteor?
by Will Murray 2
"And Shadowed On A Screen..."
H.P. Lovecraft and Cinema in his Day and Ours
by Ross Byrne 8
Musings on the Mythos
by Will Murray 14
Islam and the Middle East in the writings of H. P.
Lovecraft: Sources and Influences
by J. J. Little 17
What Would H. P. Lovecraft Have Thought About UFOs?
by Donald R. Burleson 39
HPL—Pioneer Fan
by Will Murray 44
Fun Guys from Yuggoth
The Cryptic Interview: Will Murray
by Darrell Schweitzer 48
Fun Guys from Yuggoth
The Cryptic Interview: David E. Schultz
by Darrell Schweitzer 61
Another Real—Really Hard— Lovecraft Trivia Quiz
by Steven J. Mariconda 78
R'lyeh Reviews 80

What was the Black Meteor?

by Will Murray

Of all H.P. Lovecraft correspondents, the one he was most simpatico with was unquestionably Clark Ashton Smith. They shared similar interests in composing recherché verse and were both attuned to cosmic themes, a rarity in the early years of the 20th century.

Their connection was made in August, 1922. In a letter to the young California author, Lovecraft waxed enthusiastic about Smith's book of verse, *The Star-Treader and Other Poems.*

"What a world of opiate phantasy and horror is here unveiled, and what an unique power and perspective must lie behind it!" HPL raved.

Lovecraft was especially enthralled by Smith's soaring fantastic poem, *The Hashish Eater, or The Apocalypse of Evil*, remarking in a letter dated March 25, 1923, that:

I delight in your use of the *cosmos* instead of merely the *world* as a background; you can't imagine – or then again, you probably *can*—the pictures that flit through my mind at lines like

[...]
"The blind

And worm shap'd monsters of a sunless world,
With krakens of the ultimate abyss,
And Demogorgons of the outer dark...

Their correspondence only grew in intensity over the years. By the time they were sharing the pages of *Weird Tales*, Smith and Lovecraft freely swapped imaginary gods and eldritch entities, invoking them in one another's stories and giving rise to what subsequently arose to become infamous as the Cthulhu Mythos. "Smith constantly mentions my gods, & I constantly mention his," HPL told Emil Petaja in a May 31, 1935 letter.

In one area, they diverged sharply. That was the arena of the supernatural, which we today call the paranormal.

Lovecraft was a strict materialist and rationalist, while Smith was much more open-minded on the subject.

Lovecraft arrived at his materialism through a life-long process of deep study and self-reflection coupled with self-discipline. Early in his life, he was a fantasy-prone personality who claimed to worship the Greek gods and who experienced intense, hyper-realistic nightmares involving imaginal creatures he dubbed "night-gaunts."

Smith, on the other hand, was what we would today call an "experiencer," a man with a mystical bent who sometimes encountered the strange and uncanny.

Nothing better contrasts their divergent points of view than Smith's account of two weird personal experiences, which he recounted in an undated letter from late 1933:

Of course, it would seem that the arguments of material science are pretty cogent. Perhaps it is only my innate romanticism that makes me at least hopeful that the Jeans and Einstein's have overlooked something. If ever I have the leisure and opportunity, I intend some first-hand investigation of obscure phenomena. Enough inexplicable things have happened in my own experience to make me wonder. I am pretty sure that I saw apparitions in my childhood; one instance remaining especially vivid in memory. The phantasm was that of a bowed and muffled woman, weeping or at least sorrow-stricken, which appeared one night in a corner of my bedroom in an old house which my parents had rented for several months. It certainly left an eerie impression. An-

other queer happening, of a totally different kind, occurred four or five years ago. A woman-friend and I were out walking one night in a lane near Auburn, when a dark, lightless and silent object passed over us against the stars with projectile-like speed. The thing was too large and swift for any bird, and gave precisely the effect of a *black* meteor. I have often wondered what it was. Charles Fort, no doubt, would have made a substantial item out of it for one of his volumes.

Smith's black meteor sounds suspiciously like what we would today call an Unidentified Flying Object, or Unidentified Aerial Phenomena. More data would be illuminating, but alas impossible to attain at this late date.

Reports of unusual objects sighted in the sky date back centuries. Many of these sightings have been cataloged. A search of various online databases show no sightings that match Smith's report of a black meteor passing over California, in either 1928 or 29, the likeliest years, according to his recollection.

However, in 1927 two such reports are found. The first occurred in February, in Sausalito. A woman saw a cigar-shaped object over the bay, traveling at high speed, ruling out a conventional airship. However, this object was yellow in color.

On October 18, an otherwise-undescribed "object" was observed in Bakersfield. Estimated at 80 feet across, it was observed in the desert, but it was not soundless. A noise was heard. Further details of this object are absent. Sausalito lies approximately 125 miles southwest of Auburn, while Bakersfield is 300 miles south, near San Francisco. But distances may be meaningless when dealing with fast-traveling objects of unknown origin.

If Smith's experience actually dates to 1927, the Sausalito sighting is the likeliest equivalent. Again, there are insufficient facts to make a strong determination. And it's equally probable that no other report of Smith's uncanny sighting was ever recorded.

More data would be fascinating, but not discoverable in our century.

Smith could not have seen an actual meteor fall. Meteorites are colorfully incandescent and often give off sparks as they descend. A misperceived aircraft is possible, one imagines. However, propeller-driven aircraft were quite noisy in those days, and Smith specifically notes the absence any motor sounds, leading one to believe the mysterious object was either silent, or too quiet in operation to be heard at the distance at which Smith witnessed it. The absence of structural wings is also telling.

A conventional meteor was witnessed in the skies over Fresno and Hanford in the early evening of July 27, 1927, while it was still light. However, this bolide was described as resembling a huge fireball which left a lingering smoky trail in its wake. Residents of nearby Portersville reported that the meteorite exploded while still airborne, displaying a blue electrical sputter near the end of its descent. The facts of this spectacular sighting do not match Smith's eerie black soundless body.

In response to Smith's bizarre accounts, Lovecraft responded on November 18:

> As for possible deviations from natural law as now understood—of course, one need not be dogmatic; but it seems as if all the scraps of alleged evidence for such deviations were slight, rare & highly susceptible of other explanation, as ranged against an overwhelming mass of data in the light of which they appear wildly improbable. The unreliable registration of the human senses, & the effective imagination or careless attention upon human perception, are among the most salient facts in nature—& we have seen too many marvelous myths & apparent certainties analyzed into delusions to feel sure of anything not surviving the test of rigorous investigation. I have often *thought* I witnessed marvels, yet have

invariably traced them in the end to natural components & imagination-induced visions. Thus when I was 7 years old I *positively saw* some fauns & dryads in a mystical oaken grove (still unchanged, Yuggoth be thanked!) not far from my house. But they looked *very* like the pictures in the edition of Bullfinch's Age of Fable over which I had had been avidly pouring! That muffled weeper of your own childhood was certainly a curious impression. As for the Black Meteor—all sorts of theories might be offered. A cloud—a huge kite—a dirigible adrift—Anyway, I'd go over the list of possible normal causes pretty thoroughly before adopting a Charles Fortean explanation.

Lovecraft's skeptical explanations for the aerial object are disappointingly thin and unsatisfactory. A cloud caught in the wind would not behave like a projectile, any more than a paper kite would. As for a dirigible, such as the *Graf Zeppelin*— which overflew San Francisco before docking at Los Angeles in the summer of 1929—the shape is wrong and an airship of that size would display running lights at night, never mind the inexplicable absence of sound emanating from its five 12-cylinder engines.

The sorrowful woman apparition is entirely another matter. I note that HPL does not offer any possible rational explanations. But Smith is clear that this was only one of several such experiences he has had. Taking him at his word, Clark Ashton Smith might be classified as mediumistic by disposition.

Writing to August Derleth on December 10, 1931, Lovecraft reflected on the persistence and folly of continued reports of so-called "occult" phenomena, during which he opined:

> Most people, irritated by men's real insignificance and helplessness in the cosmos, ardently wish that a spiritual world existed to give them the unreal importance formally assured them by religion. Natural limitations of time, space, and natural law are galling to them—especially in the light of the delusive and grandiloquent tradition on which they were suckled—and some consciously take to weird fiction, whilst others prefer to kid themselves along and cling to a vestigial love of the obsolescent spiritual mythology. The subconscious strength of this wish is often so great as to become translated into downright hallucination, causing the subject to experience illusionary evidences of the supernatural, or even to construct elaborate day-dreams of occultism revolving around himself.

Except for a bent toward weird fiction—a trait Smith shared with HPL—this hardly sounds like a fair description of the unreligious Clark Ashton Smith, and it's difficult to imagine that Lovecraft saw his fellow cosmic visionary in such a poor light, but Smith never belabored his experiences or attempted to convince Lovecraft of the validity of them. Between them, the subject was soon a closed one.

In the same letter in which he first told of the black meteor, Smith went on to say:

> The modern explanation of the growth of myths and superstitions is certainly well worked out. Yet, after all, it is possible that brand new psychological theories may in time supersede much that is now regarded as self-evident. Also, there is a fascinating possibility that human beings may in time develop new senses or faculties that will take them a little further into the cosmic penetralia; though, of course, never approaching ultimates or near-ultimates. It may then be suspected that the sources of human thought lie deeper and remoter than has been supposed. We are *not insulated* from the myriad unknown forces of the cosmos that play upon us; and, after all who knows what the *real* affect of

these forces may be?

In response, Lovecraft allowed:

> What do you say of *new senses* is certainly worthy of profound reflection. Certainly, our view of nature is purely subjective & fragmentary one, depending on the meagre sensory equipment called forth by an evolution whose only object is physical survival, not knowledge & perception. That is, the only links we have with the external world are special faculties designed for a very (intellectually) narrow end & having no reference to the process of envisioning or experiencing the cosmos in its totality, or even a forming an approximately full idea of the small section within our conceivable grasp. While nothing in our normal experience is ever likely to call forth any additional senses, it is not impossible that experiments with the ductless glands might open up a fresh sensitivity or two—& then what impressions might not pour in?

Lovecraft went on to observe:

> However, a vast deal might be learnt concerning the *mechanism & operation of thought*—just what modifications of tissue are involved, what transformations of energy occur,

whether any wave-motion (rendering telepathy—which is probably an unfounded legend—possible) exists in addition to molecular changes, & whether such a thing as hereditary memory can exist.

Here we see a glimpse of open-mindedness in regards to certain otherwise-"occult" phenomena. Elsewhere, Lovecraft correctly remarked, "One must use caution in accepting novel data."

Experiencers might counter with the observation that the history of science vs. the paranormal can be reduced to this observation: Skeptics who do not experience the paranormal solemnly informing people who report paranormal experiences that paranormal experiences do not exist.

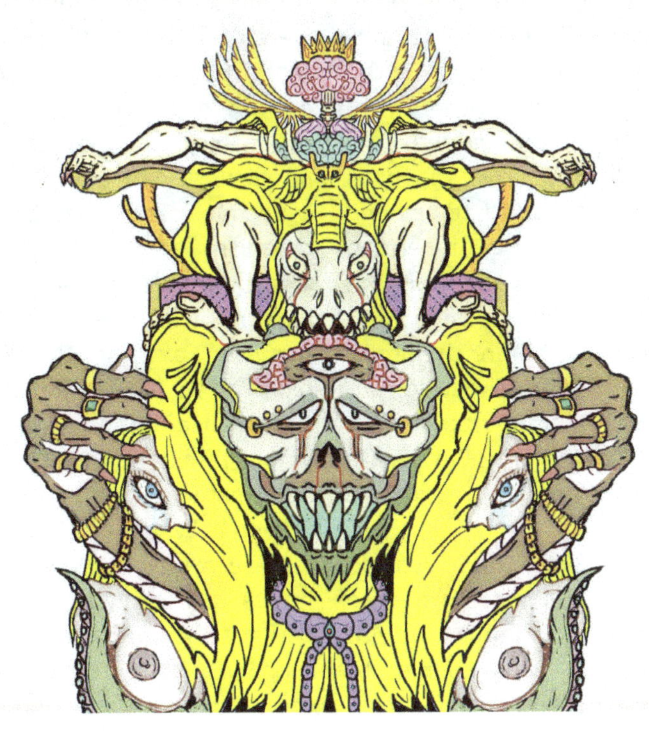

"And Shadowed On A Screen..."
H.P. Lovecraft and Cinema in his Day and Ours

by Ross Byrne

With every decade since the death of Howard Phillips Lovecraft, the field of Horror in all its forms has gradually come to be fascinated with the works of the Providence visionary. In recent times this has been at its most prominent, perhaps, in visual media, in art, drawings, comics, and Cinema, an area which had held aloof from HPL for the longest time, given the somewhat sniffy attitude of serious, weighty, art house cinema to the Horror genre, which it viewed with some suspicion and indeed condescension. While the Universal monsters of the 1930s had become iconic, and the heights of German Expressionism found easy favour in the growing literature of film studies, this was long before the proliferation of B-movies, cheap formulaic slashers and jump-scares which kept many serious critics in a state of snooty indifference towards the genre.

Of course, since the 1970s, we have gratefully witnessed the rise of a generation of filmmakers with the talent, vision and abilities to convey more depth and substance, e.g., the layering of social and political elements into George Romero's *Night of the Living Dead*, John Carpenter's films, Wes Craven's *Last House on the Left*, and Kubrick's *The Shining*. Many of the old blinders have been cast off; audiences and critics alike have reconsidered their hasty dismissals. Instead, they have come to appreciate that Horror films can engage with important human ideas and events. This is largely thanks to individual writers who saw how bigger themes could be expressed and that there weren't any barriers to exploring real art in the Macabre. And that all stretches back to Lovecraft.

In his monumental essay, *Supernatural Horror in Literature*, Lovecraft traced the roots of the organism to European folklore, world mythologies, and the steady stream of writings from the *Gilgamesh Epic* and the *1.001Arabian Nights* to the titans like Poe, which all pointed to the timeless innate fascination with the darker, nightmarish side of human imagination. While this was the perfect vessel to express everything he wanted to say in writing, Lovecraft had an understandably dimmer view of its manifestations in the movies of his era. Two of the aforementioned Universal monster icons, James Whale's *Frankenstein* and Tod Browning's *Dracula*, didn't manage to tickle his fancy, in large degree due to their changes to the source material. Having a high regard for Shelley's and Stoker's classics, he disliked the trimmings and alterations needed for the screen, especially with the censorship codes in force and the limited running times available for directors then. Lovecraft chafed at the tighter strictures of early cinema and, though initially more optimistic, HPL lost some of his high expectations for it. Nonetheless, he kept an open mind to the medium's potential. Hearing of *The Cabinet of Dr Caligari*, Weine's surreal story of a deranged mesmerist unleashing a sleepwalking killer in a German mountain town, Lovecraft was intrigued, writing to August Derleth that "Speaking of the cinema – it is my deepest regret that I never saw the *The Cabinet of Dr. Caligari*, which everyone tells me had more of the truly weird & fantastic than any other film ever made."

Hoping to see it on its arrival in Providence, busy with his work and other interests, Lovecraft never saw the film, which is a pity. Given the effect of certain powerful films on his imagination, like the charming time travel fantasy *Berkeley Square* (on which more below), we might have gotten a memorable story from such a viewing of *Caligari*. Nor was the cinema entirely absent from his prose works. In the eponymous 1920 tale that introduced readers to his entity Nyarlathotep, the unnamed narrator wanders through the streets, feeling drawn to a screening hosted by the strangely enigmatic being, depicting a series of apocalyptic disasters, ecological upheaval, and growing chaos in some near-future date. Clearly, while it was hardly a rival to his love of the written word, Lovecraft was not immune to the charms of the silver screen. If we want to explore what sort of films he responded to, there is a wealth of information in his famously voluminous correspondence, the nearly 20,000 surviving letters he sent to friends and colleagues all over America. His epistles to three or four people in particular, J. Vernon Shea, his original literary executor R.H. Barlow, and his aunt Lillian Clarke, have an abundance of information on his visits to the movies, his likes and dislikes, and those actors and filmmakers he found of interest.

The groundbreaking legends of the medium include F.W. Murnau, Fritz Lang, D.W. Griffith, Ernst Lubitsch, Rupert Julian, Todd Browning, and Cecil B. De Mille. Lovecraft saw films from each, although in the case of Murnau it wasn't *Nosferatu*, unfortunately. He did, however, see the acclaimed horror *The Golem*, initially finding in its eerie Expressionist sets and its central motif of ritual magic a memorable use of horror and fantasy. But by the time he read Meyrink's original novel, lent to him by R.H. Barlow, he revised his opinion heavily, "The cinema of the same title which I saw in 1921 was a mere substitute using the empty name: with nothing of the novel in it." An even higher regard for Stoker's *Dracula* caused him to storm out of a Miami theater. Clearly, Lovecraft's passionate absorption in the supernatural created to have very high standards for on-screen horrors, atmosphere being for him paramount. When the films dealt with more human, realist subjects, his guard was down, and he was more inclined to praise the works on their own terms. On Murnau's *The Last Laugh*, starring the acclaimed Emil Jannings as a hotel porter, he remarked, "we saw that much discussed German film, *The Last Laugh*. It is really a very powerful & pathetic short story, presented in a highly artistic & semi-impressionistic fashion, of a poor old porter as age breaks him down to the level of a basement lavatory-cleanerin a hotel. The irony is strong but subtle, & the whole well deserving of the critical panegyrick it hath receiv'd."

He had a long-term fondness for fantasy — particularly the arabesque fantasy of the *Arabian Nights* he'd discovered as a boy. He very much enjoyed *The Thief of Baghdad*, directed by Raoul Walsh and starring Douglas Fairbanks, Jr., finding in its timeless spectacles an echo of one of his literary idols. "That had a really Dunsanian touch in its Arabesque scenic setting." He went to see it more than once, in fact writing to his aunt, "Tonight S H (Sonia Haft Greene) & I will probably see *The Thief of Baghdad*, she for the first time & I for the second."

From instances like this we can draw a general impression of Lovecraft's tastes in fantasy and horror films. He had a similar response to Fritz Lang's Nibelungen film *Siegfried*, another great silent mythic tale which inspired the following ringing review from the Providence dreamer: "As for the film—it was an ecstasy & a delight to be remembered for ever! It was the very inmost soul of the immortal & unconquerable blond Nordic, embodied in the shining warrior of light, great Siegfried, slayer of monsters & enslaver of Kings. The central figure was acted by a German of perfectly adapted colouring & physique —Paul Richter—& the scenery was an absolute triumph of Northern phantasy worthy of Dunsany. Great & mysterious forests spread out with their titan trees, creeping roots, & fantastick play of light & shadow. Castles of mystery crowned haunted crags, & in the Icelandick scenes the abode of Brunhilde was a portentous wonder in colossal lava, brooding spectral & desolate under never-dying auroras." Every aspect of Lang's work seemed to affect him, right down to the score, a facet towards which he was in general, less responsive.

The musick, too, was of ineffable inspiration. Insensible as I am to musick in general, I cannot escape the majesty of Wagner, whose genius caught the deepest spirit of those ancestral yellow-bearded lords of war & dominion before whom my own soul bows as before no others—Woden, Thor, Freyr, & the vast Alfadur—frosty blue-eyed giants worthy of the adoration of a conquering people! I am certain that Wagner is the supreme musical genius of the last hundred years, at least; & perhaps the creator of the second-greatest artistick monument of the whole Nordic race, the Gothick cathedral being the greatest. Exalted beyond words, we left the theatre at last, as the funeral march of the golden-haired young demi-god pealed from the orchestra. Nothing had so inspired me in weeks, & I believe a masterful demon-tale could be founded from the sinister bass music of *Rheingold* alone!

Considering the role *Berkeley Square* played in the writing of "The Shadow out of Time," it's tempting to speculate what tale he could have spun from that.

It wasn't just cinematic fiction that he occasionally enjoyed, but also documentaries, such as *Man of Aran*, a 1934 film about the difficult lives of Aran islanders off the West Coast of Ireland who survived by "hunting titan sharks for their oil... toiling feverishly & heroically for no reward other than the precarious maintenance of physical life... The Arans have fascinated me since I read Synge's *Riders to the Sea*. Well – it's a great film, & I advise you not to miss it if you haven't seen it already," he told his young protege R. H. Barlow. Lovecraft was by no means ignorant of the power of the movies, as a whole medium, and it is to be hoped that filmmakers today can go beyond the more obvious tropes of Lovecraftian fiction — Cthulhu, the *Necronomicon*, the lamentable period racism -- in their future explorations of the genre. Certainly, some very high-profile filmmakers over the years, from actors like Christopher Lee, Vincent Price, screenwriters Dan O'Bannon and Arthur C. Clarke, and writer-directors like the genius Stanley Kubrick, have been keen Lovecraft readers, Kubrick himself referring to HPL as "The Great Master" when discussing his approach to depicting horror in *The Shining*. Indeed, Kubrick's method of absorbing elements of Lovecraft's writings into his own ideas, as he did with King's novel, is one which seems to hold more promise than direct adaptations, as good as those can be. This was also the route taken by Ridley Scott, Dan O'Bannon, and H.R. Giger with the first *Alien* film, which seems highly resonant with

a Lovecraftian atmosphere and has endured in its power to terrify new audiences. S.T. Joshi tends to concur, holding that when writers and other artists use Lovecraft as a springboard for their own imaginations, the results are often both more refreshing and more rewarding. A recent German film called *Die Farbe*, has been singled out by Joshi as one of the very few adaptations he can wholeheartedly recommend to viewers.

To return to Horror, though, there are further pointers towards the kind of screen weirdness Lovecraft responded to, like *The Phantom of the Opera*, Rupert Julian's classic starring Lon Chaney, which famously features a color sequence based on his idol Edgar Allen Poe's "Masque of the Red Death," and which worked its dark spell on the Providence visionary sitting in his theater seat.

Then the second part began -- horror lifted its grisly visage -- & I could not have been made drowsy by all the opiates under heaven! Ugh!!! The face that was revealed when the mask was pulled off... & the nameless legion of things that cloudily appeared beside & behind the owner of that face when the mob chased him into the river at the last!

As we see, he could surely appreciate the work of monster make-up artists, as he did once again when viewing *Island of Lost Souls* (movie version of *The Island of Dr. Moreau*), "which had quite a bit of fantastic horror left in it (especially the faces of the Things & their prowlings & ritual in the grotesque tropic night)."

It took a rare screen presence like Charles Laughton's to elicit much praise from Lovecraft, as he remarked to a correspondent, aspiring stage actor Lee White.

Like you, I deplore the inability of cinema performers to sink themselves in their parts. I agree concerning the merits of Charles Laughton, whom I have seen as Nero, Henry VIII, Dr. Moreau, Edward Moulton-Barrett & Inspector Javert. His Henry was surely magnificent, & his Nero scarcely less distinctive in its way.

In the present landscape of Cinema, where Horror seems to be enjoying a grand resurgence in both popular and critical esteem, with a greater focus on concept, atmosphere, acting and script, than in previous stalk-and-slash periods, as people like Joss Whedon, with his self-aware and cineliterate *Cabin in the Woods*, Jennifer Kent's return of the repressed fable *The Babadook*, and Jordan Peele's forthcoming adaptation *Lovecraft Country* are showing, we see the great advantages of bringing the same layers of meaning to a supernatural tale as you would any other genre of film, and the field is certainly reaping the benefits of it.

It's in the reinterpretation and literary mutations that the form of the weird tale survives, thrives, and replicates itself in the minds of readers and viewers, transmitting the author's intentions to the mind's eye of a culture at large. In exploring our fears and speculations on the Cosmos, which have entranced stargazers and writers of Cosmic Horror for centuries, it is Lovecraft who has been largely responsible for the rocketing popularity of the subgenre and its absorption into almost every corner of pop-culture today. A strange fate for someone whose creative ideals meant that for him writing was never about the widest success and money, often to his own detriment, but while unexpected it may have amused him to contemplate in his more cynical moments. As our societies face impending climate change and psychological readjustment to the omnipresence of the Internet, the unsettlingly prescient creations of the Old Gent from Rhode Island seem better metaphors than in their own day for what we as a species must learn to contend with. Cinema being one of the most notable conduits for our notion of ourselves, we can look forward to an unflinching future of storytelling, "radiant with beauty" as he described the allure of the Weird, and reflecting the eternal fascination of these visions.

Musings on the Mythos

by Will Murray

Decades ago, I was so bold as to assert in the august pages of Necronomicon Press' *Lovecraft Studies* a radical theory about the Cthulhu Mythos.

My theory with simple: H.P. Lovecraft wrote only three pure Mythos stories doing his two-short career. I enumerated them: "The Call of Cthulhu," "The Dunwich Horror," and "The Colour Out of Space." One could actually argue that the last tale is not necessarily an explicit exploration of the Mythos. But neither is it corrupted by outside influences. Its cosmic subject matter is comfortably Cthulhuvian.

My reasoning was as elementary as my theory. Lovecraft had no sooner commenced forming his unique cycle of myth than his *Weird Tales* compadres commenced borrowing and exploiting his concepts in stories of their own, beginning with Frank Belknap Long's 1929 story, "The Hounds of Tindalos," and continuing with Clark Ashton Smith, Robert E. Howard, and others, ransacking HPL's tales for cosmic creatures and concepts as they came along. The Old Gentleman was only too happy to indulge them, and merrily borrowed from their growing works, producing a

collaborative Cthulhu Mythos. But he eventually came to a point after a few years where he became unhappy with his own work and, rightly or wrongly, felt he had gotten off the track.

I propounded and expounded upon my theory in an article entitled "An Uncompromising Look at the Cthulhu Mythos." It appeared in *Lovecraft Studies* #12, Spring 1986.

Immediately, a great deal of controversy ensued, both pro and con. The subject was revisited at a panel at a 1986 Necon, which was transcribed and ultimately printed in the pages of *Lovecraft Studies* #14, Spring 1987, under the title, "What is the Cthulhu Mythos?"

Eventually, the minor literary tempest died down. But that was not the end of it. In 1990, publisher Philippe Gindre elected to reprint the article in a French-language chapbook and I was invited to write an introduction.

This introduction has never appeared in English, so I thought it would be interesting to revisit the subject and turn it into an article for the benefit of *Crypt of Cthulhu* readers who have been deprived of my last word on the subject.

Herewith, my introduction to *Qu'est-ce que le Mythe de Cthulhu?*, with some modest edits:

I suppose this is as good a time as any to make a confession.

When I wrote my 1986 *Lovecraft Studies* article, "An Uncompromising Look at the Cthulhu Mythos," I wasn't quite serious. In fact, my tongue was firmly in my cheek when I began writing the piece. I deliberately took an extreme position—that there were really only three genuine undiluted Cthulhu Mythos stories—to inject controversy into the otherwise staid pages of *Lovecraft Studies*. S. T. Joshi and I felt the magazine could use some excitement.

A funny thing happened while writing the article. My tongue came out of my cheek and as I wrote on, my admittedly absurd position seemed more and more plausible to me.

The article did, of course, accomplish what it was intended to do. Dave Schultz rebutted it with his thoughtful "Who Needs the Cthulhu Mythos?" and the controversy was eventually bruited about rather boisterously during a 1986 Lovecraft panel whose transcript was eventually printed in *Lovecraft Studies.*

I must say that I, as well as S.T., Bob Price and others, were sur-

prised by the tremendous popular response to our musings and mutterings, not only in the pages of *Lovecraft Studies* but internationally. We must have struck a chord for, Philippe Gindre's Le Clef d'Argent (Argent Press) reprinted it and all related *Lovecraft Studies* articles of response in a handsome chapbook back in the 1986, assuring a new edition in 2007.

But that was long ago and far away. I found it necessary to reacquaint myself with the original articles in order to pen this modest update. So many articles and novels have emerged from my computer since those halcyon days that I'd forgotten much of what we had discussed during our politely-contentious panel.

We all rather thought that while the controversy over the nature of the Cthulhu Mythos would last longer than the natural spans of our lives, we had said most of what we could expound on the subject.

I still think that. The all-pervasive interconnectedness of Lovecraft's fiction begs that the term Cthulhu Mythos be retired in favor of a suitably all-inclusive appellation like S.T. Joshi's suggested Lovecraft Mythos. But I doubt this will happen. "Cthulhu Mythos" has become indelibly ingrained in our minds, and I doubt it will ever be superseded by any more appropriate but less exotic coining.

I've not taken my researches on this point further, but a recent rereading of Lovecraft's last major story, "The Shadow Out of Time," has caused me to tentatively reassess my harsh judgement that only "The Call of Cthulhu," "The Dunwich Horror" and "The Colour Out of Space" are the only pure Mythos stories Lovecraft—or anyone— ever wrote.

I think we can add this story to the select group. My reason for thinking this has to do with the brief mention of the legend of Buddai, which Lovecraft ascribes to Australian aborigines, but which I believe he himself invented. The legend is simple, Buddai is a giant sleeping old man who will one day wake from his prolonged subterranean slumber to devour the world.

The similarities between Buddai and Cthulhu are obvious: Buddai seems to be a land-based version of the primal Cthulhu myth, stripped of its exotic impedimenta and mentioned only in passing. It's apparently dropped into the story to foreshadow the predicted awakening of the wind creatures said to lurk under Australia's Great Sandy desert during the tale's climax.

Prior to composing this story, Lovecraft had complained to his correspondents about having gotten off the track with his fiction, that for too long he had been pandering to common editorial tastes. I think with this story, which mentions few Mythos elements and Cthulhu not at all—he was beginning to return to his roots.

The fact that these wind beings are not given a Mythosesque name is indicative of Lovecraft's latterly attempt to avoid coining that which could be carried off by friendly would-be contributors to the Cthulhu Mythos and constitutes a decisive move by its originator to mature the Mythos. Had he lived to write a significant body of further stories, I venture to say Lovecraft would have written more tales like this one—cosmically powerful but not fanciful embroidery akin to mere compendia of a cosmic zoo.

Islam and the Middle East in the writings of H. P. Lovecraft: Sources and Influences

by J. J. Little (University of Oxford)

The short stories of the American author Howard Phillips Lovecraft (d. 1937) arguably redefined the genres of horror fiction and sci-fi horror during the early 20th Century, and have since exerted a significant influence upon global popular culture, including literature, cinema, television, and video games. Conversely, Lovecraft himself was influenced by a wide array of historical and cultural sources in the composition of his fiction, including numerous elements relating to Islam and the Middle East.[1] What follows is a catalogue of and commentary on some of Lovecraft's notable Islamic and Middle-Eastern references, in both his fiction and other writings.

To be clear, this is not a study of Lovecraft's *attitudes* towards Islam and the Middle East. Lovecraft's open white supremacy, xenophobia, defence of slavery, defence of lynching, and fascist sympathies are already well known and documented,[2] and it is clear that he was also an orientalist in the Saidian sense of that word: exoticising, essentialising, and stereotyping "the East" and "Easterners".[3] In-

---

1 This has been noted by many, e.g., L. Sprague de Camp, *Lovecraft: A Biography* (Garden City, USA: Doubleday & Co., Inc., 1975), 18, 165, etc.

I owe special thanks to Prof. Christopher Melchert, Dr. Robert M. Price, Dr. Marijn van Putten, and Mr. Bobby Dee for various feedback and assistance.

2 Examples of Lovecraft's bigotry are practically endless, but for a starting point, see Gavin Callaghan, *H. P. Lovecraft's Dark Arcadia: The Satire, Symbology and Contradiction* (Jefferson, USA: McFarland & Company, Inc., Publishers, 2013), ch. 6; Wes House, 'We Can't Ignore H.P. Lovecraft's White Supremacy', *Literary Hub* (26th/September/2017): https://lithub.com/we-cant-ignore-h-p-lovecrafts-white-supremacy/; Ed Power, 'The hatred of HP Lovecraft: Racist, anti-Irish bigot and horror master', *The Irish Times* (15th/August/2020): https://www.irishtimes.com/culture/tv-radio-web/the-hatred-of-hp-lovecraft-racist-anti-irish-bigot-and-horror-master-1.4326744

3 For example, when reflecting on the impact of the *Arabian Nights* in European literature and culture during the 18th Century, Lovecraft spoke of "[t]he sly humour which only the Eastern mind knows how to mix with weirdness". Concerning the Gothic novel *History of the Caliph Vathek* by William Beckford (composed in French around 1782, and translated

deed, Lovecraft's use of negative Islam-related tropes has already been studied to some degree.[4] Instead, the present article focuses on identifying and explaining the provenance of some of Lovecraft's notable *literary* and *historical* references to Islam and the Middle East.[5]

The *Arabian Nights* and Ibn Schacabao

into English and published in 1786 by Samuel Henley) in particular, which was inspired by the *Arabian Nights*, Lovecraft declared: "in his fantastic volume reflected very potently the haughty luxury, sly disillusion, bland cruelty, urbane treachery, and shadowy spectral horror of the Saracen spirit." See Howard P. Lovecraft (ed. Sunand T. Joshi), *The Annotated Supernatural Horror in Literature* (New York, USA: Hippocampus Press, 2000), 33-34.

4 Ian Almond, 'The Darker Islam within the American Gothic: Sufi Motifs in the Stories of H.P. Lovecraft', *Zeitschrift für Anglistik und Amerikanistik*, Volume 52, Issue 3 (2004), 231-242.

5 The reader should be aware that a monograph already exists that may address some of the material covered in the present article: Cédric Monget, *Lovecraft, l'Arabe, l'horreur: Orient et Islam chez le gentleman de Providence* (Dijon, France: La Clef d'Argent, 2021). Unfortunately, I only learned of this work at the last minute, and was not able to access it before publication.

Lovecraft's introduction to Islam and the Middle East ostensibly occurred around the age of five, when he started reading a famous collection of stories variously known as *One Thousand and One Nights* or *Arabian Nights*, an English translation of the famous French work *Les Mille et une nuits* (1704-1717).[6] The latter was in turn a translation by the French orientalist Antoine Galland (d. 1715) of a Syrian recension of a widespread Mediaeval corpus of popular Arabic stories—ultimately rooted in pre-Islamic (especially Persian) literature—associated with the name 'One Thousand and One Nights' ('Alf *Laylah wa-Laylah*).[7]

6 Or at least, the version accessed by Lovecraft was an English translation (Andrew Lang, 1898) of the French translation; see Sunand T. Joshi & David E. Schultz, *An H.P. Lovecraft Encyclopedia* (Westport, USA: Greenwood Press, 2001), 154. In the course of the 19th Century, various English translations made directly from Arabic recensions of the work began to appear—notably, the 1840 translation of Edward W. Lane (d. 1876), the 1882 translation of John Payne (1916), and the 1885 translation of Richard F. Burton (d. 1890).

7 For an overview, see Enno Littmann, '*Alf Layla wa-Layla*', in Hamilton A. R. Gibb, Johannes H. Kramers, Évariste Lévi-Provençal, Joseph F. Schacht, Bernard Lewis, & Charles Pellat (eds.), *The Encyclopaedia of Islam, New Edition, Volume 1: A-B* (Leiden, the Netherlands: Koninklijke

Lovecraft related his encounter with the *Arabian Nights* in his 1922 essay 'A Confession of Unfaith', as follows:

> Within the next few years I added to my supernatural lore the fairy tales of Grimm and the Arabian Nights; and by the time I was five had small choice amongst these speculations so far as truth was concerned, though for attractiveness I favoured the Arabian Nights. At one time I formed a juvenile collection of Oriental pottery and *objets d'art*, announcing myself as a devout Mussulman and assuming the pseudonym "Abdul Alhazred".[8]

The young Lovecraft's conversion to Islam was short-lived and he became an atheist soon afterwards, although he continued to appreciate "the Eastern magnifi-

cence of Mahometanism."[9]

Direct borrowings from the *Arabian Nights* manifested in Lovecraft's later work. In his 1923 short story *The Festival* (published in 1925),[10] for example, the narrator quotes the following passage from a fabled in-world tome (a Low Latin translation of the Arabic *Necronomicon*), in which the pseudo-Arabic name "Ibn Schacabao" is invoked:

> Wisely did Ibn Schacabao say, that happy is the tomb where no wizard hath lain, and happy the town at night whose wizards are all ashes.[11]

Brill NV, 1960), 358-364; Charles Pellat, 'Alf Layla wa Layla', in Ehsan Yarshater (ed.), *Encyclopaedia Iranica, Volume 1: Āb - Anāhīd* (London, UK: Routledge & Kegan Paul, 1985), 831-835.

8 Howard P. Lovecraft, 'A Confession of Unfaith', in Sunand T. Joshi (ed.), *Against Religion: The Atheist Writings of H.P. Lovecraft* (New York, USA: Sporting Gentlemen, 2010), 6.

---

9 *Ibid.*

10 Joshi & Schultz, *An H.P. Lovecraft Encyclopedia*, 92.

11 Howard P. Lovecraft, 'The Festival', in August Derleth & Sunand T. Joshi (eds.), *Dagon and Other Macabre Tales*, corrected 5th printing (Sauk

This name reappears in Lovecraft's 1927 novel *The Case of Charles Dexter Ward*, in the journal of a necromancer:

> I laste Night struck on ye Wordes that bringe up YOG-GE-SOTHOTHE, and sawe for ye first Time that Face spoke of by Ibn Schacabao in ye — —.[12]

Some mystery surrounds this pseudo-Arabic name. The provenance of "Ibn" is straightforward (being Arabic for "son", here meaning "the son of Schacabao"), but whence came "Schacabao"? Lovecraft fans, enthusiasts, and scholars have come up with several explanations over the years, summarised by Leslie Klinger as follows:

> The name "Ibn Schacabao" is mentioned again in *The Case of Charles Dexter Ward*, note 135, below. "Schacabao" is not a proper Arabic name, and the suggestion has been made that it is a corruption of *Ibn Shayk Abol* (Son of the Sheik Abol) or *Ibn Mushacab* (Son of the Dweller; *shacab* means to sit or dwell). It may also be derived from the Hebrew *shakhabh* (a sexual term connoting homosexuality or bestiality); or it may be a corruption of the Arabic name Schacabac—a poor man who appears in the tale "The Barmecide's Feast" recorded in *The Arabian Nights*.[13]

To begin with, the "Ibn Shayk Abol" suggestion is problematic in Arabic: "Shayk" (*šayk̲*, variously meaning elder, chief, master, or scholar) should be definite here (i.e., *al-šayk̲*), for "Son of the Sheik Abol" to make sense as a translation. Moreover, "Abol" (if it is Arabic at all) can only be *'abū al-*, "the father of the...", which is grammatically incorrect: if the "Son of the Sheik Abol" translation is again to stand, then *'abū* would have to be in apposition with *al-šayk̲*; but since *al-šayk̲* is the *muḍāf 'ilay-hi* in an *'iḍāfah* construct with *ibn*, it is in the genitive case, which means that *'abū* ought to be genitive as well (i.e., *'abī*). All of this could be

---

City, USA: Arkham House Publishers, 1986), 216.

12 Howard P. Lovecraft, 'The Case of Charles Dexter Ward', in M. J. Elliott (compiler), *Collected Stories, Volume 1: The Whisperer in Darkness* (Ware, UK: Wordsworth Editions, Ltd., 2007), 101.

13 Leslie S. Klinger, in Howard P. Lovecraft, *The New Annotated H. P. Lovecraft* (New York, USA: Liveright, 2014), 113, n. 37. Also see Robert M. Price, 'A Critical Commentary on the *Necronomicon*', in Robert M. Price (ed.), *The Necronomicon: Selected Stories and Essays Concerning the Blasphemous Tome of the Mad Arab* (Oakland, USA: Chaosium, Inc., 1996), 273.

avoided if we reject the English translation given above and reinterpret the hypothetical Arabic as follows, with *'abū* being in apposition with *ibn*: "son of a shaykh, father of the..." (*ibnᵘ šayk̲ⁱⁿ 'abū al-*). However, there is no getting around the deeper problem of *'abū al-*: this is nonsensical in Arabic. The definite article (*al-*) cannot be separated from its noun. Thus, "Ibn Shayk Abol" (*ibnᵘ šayk̲ⁱⁿ 'abū al-*) must be jettisoned as a possible explanation for the origin of Lovecraft's "Ibn Schacabao".

Of course, this problem can be sidestepped if we simply emend "Ibn Shayk Abol" to "Ibn Shayk Abo" (*ibnᵘ šayk̲ⁱⁿ 'abū*), which fits Lovecraft's "Ibn Schacabao" much better—but in doing so, we evade one problem by walking squarely into another. In Arabic, *'abū* (as opposed to *'ab*) has to be part of an *'iḍāfah* (e.g., *'abū fulān*, "the father of so-and-so") or given an attached pronoun (e.g., *'abū-hu*, "his father")—without either, we again have a nonsensical Arabic name. As such, the hypothetical name ("Ibn Shayk Abol") underpinning Lovecraft's "Ibn Schacabao" cannot actually derive from Arabic: it can only have been constructed by someone with a fleeting impression of (probably bad) English or other European transliterations of Arabic names. Of course, Lovecraft fits that bill: it is certainly conceivable that he constructed "Ibn Schacabao" based on a half-memory of several poorly-Anglicised Arabic names.

The second proposal for the origin of "Ibn Schacabao" is "Ibn Mushacab", which supposedly means "Son of the Dweller" and derives from the root *shacab*, meaning, "to sit or dwell". No such root (whether *š-q-b* or *š-k-b*) exists in Classical Arabic. The standard roots with these meanings are *j-l-s* ("to sit"), *q-ʿ-d* ("to sit down"), and *s-k-n* ("to dwell"), none of which have any resemblance to *"shacab"*.[14] Perhaps *"shacab"* exists somewhere in colloquial or dialectal forms of Arabic, but if so, there is certainly no reason to think that Lovecraft had access to anything relating thereto or emanating therefrom.[15]

----

14 The closest thing that a colleague of mine could think of is Form III of the *ṣ-q-b* root (e.g., *muṣāqabah*), which includes the meanings "to be neighbours" and "to be adjacent". However, as he agreed, this is a stretch: these meanings seem quite distant from "sitting" or "dwelling", and in any case, the letter *ṣād* is unlikely to be heard or rendered as "sh" (as opposed to simply "s").

15 The exception to this would be *Arabian Nights*, which is composed in what modern scholars call "Middle Arabic" (i.e., containing colloquial or dialectal influences or elements)—but there is no "Mushacab" in any English translation thereof, nor indeed in any historical source prior to the speculations of Lovecraft fans.

The third proposal for the origin of "Schacabao" is not Arabic at all, but Hebrew: the verb "shakhabh" (*šāḵaḇ*), which literally means "to lie down", but figuratively signifies homosexuality or bestiality. Lovecraft apparently had access to someone who could read Hebrew,[16] so this is at least conceivable. Still, it seems like a stretch: why would Lovecraft have drawn upon (i.e., badly paraphrased) a Hebrew word in his creation of what was supposed to be an Arabic name? After all, he had access to translations of Arabic stories, featuring all manner of Arabic names (albeit poorly Anglicised): why not draw upon this more germane reservoir of inspiration? A Hebrew origin would be unexpected, to say in the least.

The fourth and final proposal is that Lovecraft's "Ibn Schacabao" is a corruption of "Schacabac", the name of a character that appears in pre-Burton English translations of the *Arabian Nights*, following Galland's French original.[17] This is clearly the correct hypothesis: Schacabao looks exactly like a misreading of Schacabac *in the Latin alphabet* (since the "c" and the "o" can be easily mistaken, especially in early, italicised type). Moreover, it is a matter of record that Lovecraft possessed a copy of Andrew Lang's 19th-Century translation of *Arabian Nights*,[18] and further, that Joseph Addison—the author of pseudo-*Nights* stories that borrowed the name Schacabac[19]—was "one of Lovecraft's eighteenth-century idols".[20] In other words, there is no need to speculate garbled Arabic patronyms, lost Arabic roots, or a symbolic Hebrew etymology: Lovecraft had direct access to the (Gallicised) Arabic name Schacabac

---

A Plain and Literal Translation of the Arabian Nights' Entertainments. Now Entitled The Book of the Thousand Nights and a Night, Volume 1 (USA: The Burton Club, n. d.), 343. More recently, the (much more accurate) "Shaqâshiq" has appeared, as in Ulrich Marzolph, Richard van Leeuwen, & Hassan Wassouf, *The Arabian Nights Encyclopedia, Volume 1* (Santa Barbara, California: ABC CLIO, 2004), 121.

18 See above.

19 Joseph Addison, 'Nº 162 Wedneſday, September 16', in Richard Steele & Joseph Addison, *The Guardian. Volume the Second* (London, UK: Printed for Jacob and Richard Tonson, 1760), 440 ff.

20 De Camp, *Lovecraft*, 143.

---

16 Joshi & Schultz, *An H.P. Lovecraft Encyclopedia*, 302.

17 Compare Antoine Galland, *Les mille et une nuits, contes arabes. Traduits en français. Tome Cinquie'me. Troisiéme Edition, revûë & corrigée* (The Hague, the Netherlands: Pierre Husson, 1706), 113 ff.; Andrew Lang, *The Arabian Nights Entertainments* (London, UK: Longmans, Green, & Co., 1896), 209 ff. Cf. "Shakashik" in Richard F. Burton,

at an early age, and it would be truly remarkable if he had somehow independently created or rendered something nearly identical to this extremely unusual word, *and applied it in the same way* (i.e., as an Arabic name in a story). The conclusion is inescapable: the "Schacabao" in Lovecraft's "Ibn Schacabao" is a slight misreading of "Schacabac", the Gallicised name of a character in early translations of *Arabian Nights*.

As it happens, Lovecraft himself was not responsible for this corruption: as John Whelan has observed,[21] the original 1925 print of Lovecraft's *The Festival* in the American fantasy and horror magazine *Weird Tales* has "Ibn Schacabac", not "Ibn Schacabao".[22] Likewise, as Whelan again observed, the original manuscript of Lovecraft's *The Case of Charles Dexter Ward* has "Ibn Schacabac", not "Ibn Schacabao".[23] The corruption

of "Schacabac" into "Schacabao" appears to have occurred in early Arkham House editions of *The Festival*, which appears to have led the Lovecraft scholar and editor Sunand Joshi to mistakenly emend "Schacabac" to "Schacabao" in the edition of *The Case of Charles Dexter Ward* that he published in 1989. More recently, however, Joshi emended has "Schacabao" back to "Schacabac", restoring Lovecraft's original wording.[24]

What then does "Schacabac" mean? The Arabic original (šaqāšiq) derives from the unusual quadri-consonantal root š-*q*-š-*q*, which carries—according to the German British linguist and orientalist Francis Steingass—the following general meanings: "pronounce distinctly; twitter, peep; talk very glibly; roar, cry out".[25] Likewise, according to the German Arabist Hans Wehr[26] (as conveyed into English by

---

21 John Whelan, comment posted on the thread "Ibn Schacabac (not Ibn Schacabao)", in the alt.horror.cthulhu section of the Narkive Newsgroup Archive (22nd/March/2013): https://alt.horror.cthulhu.narkive.com/QIJNvU5o/ibn-schacabac-not-ibn-schacabao. I owe special thinks to Bobby Dee for directing me to this source.

22 Howard P. Lovecraft, 'The Festival', in *Weird Tales*, Volume 5, Issue 1 (January, 1925), 174, col. 2.

23 *Id.*, 'The case of Charles Dexter

Ward' (1927), p. 40. *Brown Archival & Manuscript Collections Online*. Brown Digital Repository. Brown University Library. https://repository.library.brown.edu/studio/item/bdr:310517/

24 I.e., in Howard P. Lovecraft (ed. Sunand T. Joshi), *H. P. Lovecraft's Collected Fiction: A Variorum Edition*, 3 vols. (New York, USA: Hippocampus Press, 2015).

25 Francis J. Steingass, *The Student's Arabic-English Dictionary* (London, UK: W. H. Allen & Co., 1884), 549.

26 His most notable achievement

J. Milton Cowan), the š-*q*-š-*q* root means: "to twitter, peep, chirp; to babble".[27] As for šaqāšiq in particular, this is the plural of šaqšaqah, which Wehr defined as the "faucal bag of the camel",[28] and Steingass defined as the "part of a camel's throat, which is protruded in roaring, sound produced by it; glibness of tongue; great eloquence; Persian belt".[29] How šaqāšiq became "Schacabac" in French (with the "š" in the third radical position becoming a "b") is unclear to me: the letter šīn does not resemble the letter *bā*ʾ in most Arabic scripts, so one could hardly mistake the former for the latter.[30]

In short, the Arabic word šaqāšiq (camel's faucal bag, camel's roar, etc.) was used as the name of a character in a story in the Mediaeval ʾAlf *Laylah wa-Laylah* corpus; a Syrian recension of this corpus was translated into French as *Les Mille et une nuits* by Galland in 1704-1717, in which Šaqāšiq became Schacabac; the French version was in turn translated into English as *The Arabian Nights Entertainments* by Lang in 1898, in which the Gallicised Schacabac was retained; a copy of this English translation was given to Lovecraft as a child (who also later admired Addison, a parallel borrower of Schacabac from *Les Mille et une nuits*); Schacabac was incorporated by Lovecraft (from either Lang or Addison) in his 1923 short story *The Festival*, and again in his 1927 novel *The Case of Charles Dexter Ward*, in the name of the mysterious character Ibn Schacabac; the name Ibn Schacabac was corrupted into Ibn Schacabao in certain later editions of Lovecraft's work, giving rise to all manner of fan and scholarly speculation as to the provenance thereof; and, finally, Ibn Schacabao has been restored to Ibn Schacabac in more some recent editions of Lovecraft's work.

---

was the composition of *Arabisches Wörterbuch für die Schriftsprache der Gegenwart*, which has gone on to become (via Cowan's translation) the most accessible and useful dictionary of Classical Arabic in the English language. Less known is the fact that Wehr was a member of the Nazi Party, whose dictionary project was funded by the German government during WW2 with the aim of translating *Mein Kampf* into Arabic. In retrospect, the dictionary's inclusion of the verb *tahatlara* ("to behave like, or imitate, Hitler") should have been a dead giveaway.

27 Hans B. G. Wehr (ed. J. Milton Cowan), *A Dictionary of Modern Written Arabic (Arabic – English)*, 4th ed. (Urbana, USA: Spoken Language Services, Inc., 1994), 562, col. 1.

28 *Ibid*.

29 Steingass, *The Student's Arabic-English Dictionary*, 549.

---

30 However, as Dr. Marijn van Putten pointed out to me, such a mistake would be feasible in the *ruqʿah* style of Arabic script.

'Iram of the Pillars

Lovecraft's 1921 short story *The Nameless City* is set "remote in the desert of Araby",[31] and tells the tale of an explorer venturing into an ancient ruined city; the explorer recalls some poetry of "Abdul Alhazred the mad poet"[32] relevant to these ruins, and notes that "the Arabs had good reason for shunning the nameless city."[33] Lovecraft also drew upon actual Arabian and Islamic mythology in this story (probably based on the entry on 'Arabia' in the 9th edition of the *Encyclopaedia Britannica*, which he possessed),[34] and has the explorer interpret a mural as depicting "a pioneer of ancient Irem, the City of Pillars."[35]

The mysterious city of 'Iram of the Pillars ('iram *ḏāt al-*'imād) was mentioned in the Quran, where it appears in connection to the ancient Arabian nation of 'Ād.[36] Although the later Islamic tradition located the people of 'Ād and their 'Iram in southern Arabia,[37] the extant evidence suggests instead that they existed in the north of the peninsula: the Nabataean ruin of '-r-m has been identified as the Quranic 'Iram, which is corroborated by Ptolemy's reference in the 2nd Century to a nation in Northwest Arabia called the "Oadites" (i.e., Aadites or people of 'Ād) and their capital "Aramaua" (i.e., 'Iram).[38]

Abdul Alhazred and the *Necronomicon*

In his 1927 *The History of the Necronomicon* (posthumously published in 1938),[39] Lovecraft outlined the fictional origins and transmission of an evil grimoire entitled *Necronomicon*, which featured

---

31 Howard P. Lovecraft, *The Dream Cycle of H.P. Lovecraft: Dreams of Terror and Death* (New York, USA: Ballantine Books, 1995), 55.

32 *Ibid.*, 55.

33 *Ibid.*

34 Joshi & Schultz, *An H.P. Lovecraft Encyclopedia*, 182.

35 Lovecraft, *The Dream Cycle*, 62.

36 Q. 89:6-8.

37 E.g., 'Ismā'īl b. 'Umar b. Kaṯīr (ed. Sāmī b. Muḥammad Salāmah), *Tafsīr al-Qur'ân al-*'Aẓīm, vol. 3 (Riyadh, KSA: Dār Ṭaybah, 1999), p. 433, *ad* Q. 7:65-69: "Their dwelling places were [located] in Yemen, in *al-*'aḥqāf, which are sand dunes."

38 Frants Buhl, ''Ād', in Hamilton A. R. Gibb, Johannes H. Kramers, Évariste Lévi-Provençal, Joseph F. Schacht, Bernard Lewis, & Charles Pellat (eds.), *The Encyclopaedia of Islam, New Edition, Volume 1: A-B* (Leiden, the Netherlands: Koninklijke Brill NV, 1960), 169; Lina Eckenstein, *A History of Sinai* (New York, USA: The MacMillan Co., 1921), 49.

39 Joshi & Schultz, *An H.P. Lovecraft Encyclopedia*, 111.

prominently in his writings. This pseudo-history draws heavily upon Middle-Eastern culture and history, since Lovecraft deemed the *Necronomicon* to have originated as an Arabic text from the early 8th Century.[40] According to Lovecraft:

> Original title *Al Azif*—*azif* being the word used by Arabs to designate that nocturnal sound (made by insects) supposed to be the howling of daemons.[41]

The "azif" cited here by Lovecraft derives from the ʿ-*z-f* root in Arabic, meaning "to whistle, howl (wind); to play (on a musical instrument; tunes); to play (to or for), make music (for s.o.)".[42] From this root comes the specific term that Lovecraft cited: ʿazīf,

meaning "whistling (of the wind); weird sound or noise", according to Wehr.[43] To this, the English orientalist Edward Lane (d. 1876) added: "the *sound of the winds in the atmosphere, imagined by the people of the desert to be the sound of the jinn*."[44] Thus, the phrase ʿazīf al-jinn can be found be found in Arabic sources and usage, sometimes in reference to the phenomenon of 'singing sands' in the desert.[45] Lovecraft undoubtedly learned of this term from Samuel Henley's notes in William Beckford's 1786 novel *Vathek*,[46] which Lovecraft read in

---

40 Howard P. Lovecraft & Willis Conover, *Lovecraft at Last* (Arlington, USA: Carrollton-Clark, 1975), 106.

41 *Ibid.* On a sidenote, Classical Arabic book titles conventionally begin with the "the book of…" (*kitāb*), which means that the *ur-Necronomicon* would probably warrant the fuller title *Kitāb al-ʿAzīf*, rather than merely *al-ʿAzīf*. This convention has been adopted in post-Lovecraftian or pseudo-Lovecraftian literature, as in the following: Abdul Alhazred, *Al Azif* (Philadelphia, USA: Owlswick Press, 1973), vii: "…Alhazred's celebrated *Necronomicon*, or *Kitab Al-Azif* to give it its original title."

42 Wehr (trans. Cowan), *Arabic-English Dictionary*, 714, col. 1.

43 *Ibid.*

44 Edward W. Lane, *An Arabic-English Lexicon* (Beirut, Lebanon: Librairie du Liban, 1968), 2035, col. 2.

45 E.g., Ignaz Goldziher (ed. Samuel M. Stern and trans. Christa R. Barber & Samuel M. Stern), *Muslim Studies, Volume 2* (Albany, USA: State University Press of New York, 1971), 53; Ramzi Baalbaki, 'The place of al-Jahiz in the Arabic philological tradition', in Arnim Heinemann, John L. Meloy, Tarif Khalidi, & Manfred Kropp (eds.), *Al-Jāḥiẓ: A Muslim Humanist for our Time* (Beirut, Lebanon: Orient-Institut Berlin, 2009), 96; Nefeli Papoutsakis, *Desert Travel as a Form of Boasting: A Study of Ḏū a-Rumma's Poetry* (Wiesbaden, Germany: Otto Harrassowitz GmbH & Co. KG, 2009), 60.

46 As Edward Ross noted in William T. Beckford (trans. Samuel Henley and annot. Edward D. Ross), *The History of the Caliph Vathek*

July of 1921.[47] Beckford referred to "the sullen hum of those nocturnal insects which presage evil,"[48] and Henley specified in the endnotes that "the nocturnal sound called by the Arabians azif was believed to be the howling of demons."[49]

(Edinburgh, UK: Morrison & Gibb Ltd., 1900), xxx, the history of Beckford's *Vathek* is confusing and obscure: the book was first commenced by Beckford in French in 1782, during the course of which he corresponded with his friend Henley; the latter (instigated by the former) translated this French original into English, and "prepared the notes thereto with Beckford's aid"; in 1786, Henley (against the wishes of Beckford, who wanted to delay publication) published his English translation of *Vathek*; however, most early editions of these works were somehow lost, as Ross (*ibid.*) noted: "Few facts in connection with Vathek are more strange than the almost entire disappearance of the first three editions, which are to-day represented by about a dozen copies in all." For a relatively early extant edition of this work, see: William Beckford (trans. Samuel Henley), *Vathek*, 3rd ed., revised and corrected (London, UK: W. Clarke, 1816).

47 Sunand T. Joshi, *H.P. Lovecraft: A Life* (West Warwick, USA: Necronomicon Press, 1996), 285. Also see Joshi & Schultz, *An H.P. Lovecraft Encyclopedia*, 186-187.

48 Beckford, *Vathek* (1816), 82-83.

49 The 1816 edition of *Vathek* actually lacks this annotation; the

Lovecraft continued:

Composed by Abdul Alhazred, a mad poet of Sanaá, in Yemen, who is said to have flourished during the period of the Ommiade caliphs, circa 700 A.D.[50]

The name "Abdul Alhazred" originated either as a nickname bestowed upon Lovecraft by a relative as a child, or else from young Lovecraft's own imagination.[51] The name is of course famously nonsense,[52] since it reduplicates the

---

earliest that I can find is the following: William Beckford (trans. Samuel Henley), *Vathek: An Arabian Tale* (London, UK: Richard Bentley, 1836), 113. However, an earlier book—Stephen Weston, *Moral Aphorisms in Arabic, and a Persian Commentary in Verse, translated from originals. With Specimens of Persian Poetry. Likewise additions to the author's conformity of the Arabic and Persian with the English Language* (London, UK: S. Rousseau, 1805), 96—actually contains near-identical text to this annotation, under the heading "Notes on some Arabic words in Vathek": "P. 245. And the nocturnal found [sic], called by the Arabians, azif."

50 Lovecraft & Conover, *Lovecraft at Last*, 106.

51 Sunand T. Joshi, *A Dreamer and a Visionary: H.P. Lovecraft in His Time* (Liverpool, UK: Liverpool University Press, 2001), 17-18.

52 Noted in Edgar Hoffmann Price, *Book of the Dead: Friends of*

Despite these linguistic difficulties, the fictional biography affixed to Abdul Alhazred has historical verisimilitude: the city of Ṣanʿāʾ was the provincial capital of Yemen under the Umayyad dynasty, who reigned until the 740s from their imperial capital Damascus.[57]

---

of the mad Arab Abdul Alhazred, then we must read these last three syllables for precisely what they say: 'all has read', that which has been read by everybody..." Likewise, Daniel Harms & John Wisdom Gonce III, *Necronomicon Files: The Truth Behind Lovecraft's Legend*, rev. & expanded ed. (Boston, USA: Weiser Books, 2003), 5, 88. In other words, the name is a pun *in English*, resulting (in conjunction with "Abdul") in "The Slave/Servant of All Has Read". This seems like a stretch to me: "Alhazred" looks like exactly the kind of thing that an English speaker would invent if they were attempting to mimic Arabic without knowing Arabic, and although Lovecraft discusses the origins of the name at several points, he never mentioned this pun etymology. Again, it seems to me simpler to suppose that it is pseudo-Arabic gibberish, but *allāh ʾaʿlam.*

57 For the Umayyads and Ṣanʿāʾ respectively, see: Gerald R. Smith, 'Ṣanʿāʾ", in Clifford E. Bosworth, Emeri J. van Donzel, Wolfhart P. Heinrichs, & Gerard Lecomte (eds.), *The Encyclopaedia of Islam, New Edition, Volume 9: San-Sze* (Leiden, the Netherlands: Koninklijke Brill NV, 1997), 1-3; and Gerald R. Hawting, 'Umayyads', in Peri J. Bearman, Thierry Bianquis, Clifford E. Bosworth, Emeri

definite article (*al-*)—literally, "the servant/slave of the the hazred". Some have thus attempted to salvage this name by emending it to something "more idiomatic" like Abd el-Hazred,[53] but even this version suffers from the simple fact that "Hazred" is not an Arabic word.[54] The closest thing I can think of is *ḥaḍrah* ("presence", often used as a title of respect),[55] which has often entered English via Urdu as "Hazrat". This is conceivable, although it is puzzling that the "at" in the Anglicised "Hazrat" became "ed" in Lovecraft's mind (or the mind of his relative). Childhood whimsy, or mere error, could always be invoked, but it seems simpler to suppose that "Alhazred" is simply some pseudo-Arabic gibberish that Lovecraft or a relative came up with when he was young.[56]

Yesteryear: Fictioneers & Others (Sauk City, USA: Arkham House Publishers, 2001), 63-64, and many other sources.

53 Joshi & Schultz, *An H.P. Lovecraft Encyclopedia*, 186.

54 Also see Price, *Book of the Dead*, 63-64.

55 Wehr (trans. Cowan), *Arabic-English Dictionary*, 215, col. 2.

56 Some have suggested that "Alhazred" should be read as "all has read", e.g., David Punter, *Gothic Pathologies: The Text, the Body and the Law* (Houndmills, UK: Macmillan Press, Ltd., 1998), 2: "When even a pulp writer like H.P. Lovecraft speaks obsessively of the Necronomicon

Lovecraft continued further:

He visited the ruins of Babylon and the subterranean secrets of Memphis and spent ten years alone in the great southern desert of Arabia—the Roba el Khaliyeh or "Empty Space" of the ancients and "Dahna" or "Crimson" desert of the modern Arabs, which is held to be inhabited by protective evil spirits and monsters of death. Of this desert many strange and unbelievable marvels are told by those who pretend to have penetrated it.[58]

Lovecraft's references to the deserts of the Arabia are again apposite: the southern portion of the peninsula is indeed dominated by a large sand desert called the Empty Quarter (*al-rub' al-ḵālī*),[59] which connects to a corridor of a dune desert called *al-dahnā'*—taken to mean "red" by some—running along the eastern coast of Arabia.[60] Additionally, the Empty Quarter in particular supposedly has a reputation for being genie-infested,[61] which fits well with Lovecraft's description.

Lovecraft continued:

In his last years Alhazred dwelt in Damascus, where the *Necronomicon* (*Al Azif*) was written, and of his final death or disappearance (738 A.D.) many terrible and conflicting things are told. He is said by Ebn Khallikan (12th century biographer) to have been seized by an invisible monster in broad daylight and devoured horribly before a large number of fright-frozen

---

J. van Donzel, & Wolfhart P. Heinrichs (eds.), *The Encyclopaedia of Islam, New Edition, Volume 10: T-U* (Leiden, the Netherlands: Koninklijke Brill NV, 2000), 840-846. The final Marwanid caliph, Marwān II (r. 744-750), moved the imperial capital to Ḥarrān in al-Jazīrah; see Géza Fehérvári, 'Ḥarrān', in Bernard Lewis, Victor L. Ménage, Charles Pellat, & Joseph F. Schacht (eds.), *The Encyclopaedia of Islam, New Edition, Volume 3: H-Iram* (Leiden, the Netherlands: Koninklijke Brill NV, 1971), 228, col. 1.

58 Lovecraft & Conover, *Lovecraft at Last*, 106.

59 Geoffrey R. D. King, 'al-Rub' al-Khālī', in Clifford E. Bosworth, Emeri J. van Donzel, Wolfhart P. Heinrichs, & Gerard Lecomte (eds.), *The Encyclopaedia of Islam, New Edition, Volume 8: Ned-Sam* (Leiden, the Netherlands: Koninklijke Brill NV, 1995), 575-576.

60 Charles D. Matthews, 'al-Dahnā', in Bernard Lewis, Charles Pellat, & Joseph F. Schacht (eds.), *The Encyclopaedia of Islam, New Edition, Volume 2: C-G* (Leiden, the Netherlands: Koninklijke Brill NV, 1965), 91-93.

61 E.g., David C. King, *Oman* (Tarrytown, USA: Marshall Cavendish Benchmark, 2009), 9-10.

witnesses.[62]

Lovecraft's citation of ʾAḥmad b. Muḥammad b. Ḵallikān (d. 1282)—despite his misidentification of the century to which Ibn Ḵallikān belonged—was particularly savvy; this Damascene scholar was famous for his *Wafayāt al-ʾAʿyān wa-ʾAnbāʾ ʾAbnāʾ al-Zamān*, an extensive and authoritative biographical dictionary of notable Muslims throughout history.[63]

Lovecraft continued further:

Of his madness many things are told. He claimed to have seen fabulous Irem, or City of Pillars, and to have found beneath the ruins of a certain nameless desert town the shocking annals and secrets of a race older than mankind. He was only an indifferent Moslem, worshipping unknown entities whom he called Yog-Sothoth and Cthulhu.[64]

As in his 1921 *The Nameless City*, Lovecraft cited the lost city of ʾIram from Arabian and Islamic mythology (explained above) and other such ruins, in which Abdul Alhazred discovered forbidden knowledge. Lovecraft's consequent description of Abdul Alhazred as "only an indifferent Moslem" is á *propos* given the perceived tendency of mystics and occultists towards blasphemy, heresy, and apostasy. For example, the infamous Muslim alchemist Jābir b. Ḥayyān (cited by Lovecraft elsewhere) allegedly "proclaimed the imminent advent of a new *imām* who would abolish the law of Islam and replace the revelation of the Ḵurʾān by the lights of Greek science and philosophy."[65]

As above with ʾIram, the ultimate source for most of this background geographical and historical information was doubtless the 9th edition of the *Encyclopaedia Britannica*, from which Lovecraft borrowed directly on several occasions.[66]

The *Qanoon-e-Islam*

In the unpublished 1927 short-novel *The Case of Charles Dexter Ward*, the narrator tells of

---

62 Lovecraft & Conover, *Lovecraft at Last*, 106.

63 Johann W. Fück, 'Ibn Ḵhallikān', in Bernard Lewis, Victor L. Ménage, Charles Pellat, & Joseph F. Schacht (eds.), *The Encyclopaedia of Islam, New Edition, Volume 3: H-Iram* (Leiden, the Netherlands: Koninklijke Brill NV, 1971), 832-833.

64 Lovecraft & Conover, *Lovecraft at Last*, 106.

65 Paul Kraus & Martin Plessner, 'Djābir b. Ḥayyān', in Lewis *et al.* (eds.), *EI²*, II, 358.

66 E.g., Joshi & Schultz, *An H.P. Lovecraft Encyclopedia*, 115, and esp. 182.

how an English gentleman named John Merritt encountered the library of a necromancer, which included a certain *Liber Investigationis* attributed to the notable Arab alchemist "Geber" (i.e., Jābir b. Ḥayyān); after listing various esoteric works, Lovecraft narrates:

> Mediaeval Jews and Arabs were represented in profusion, and Mr. Merritt turned pale when, upon taking down a fine volume conspicuously labelled as the *Qanoon-e-Islam*, he found it was in truth the forbidden *Necronomicon* of the mad Arab Abdul Alhazred...[67]

The title "Qanoon-e-Islam" cited in Lovecraft's story originated with the early 19th-Century ethnography of Indian Islam written by the Deccan physician Jaffur Shurreef; this survey was commissioned by the British surgeon Gerhard Herklots, who translated it from Hindustani into English in 1832 with the title *Qanoon-e-Islam*.[68] Subsequently, "Herklot's translation of the *Qanoon-e-Islam*" was cited in a footnote in the entry on 'Magic' in the 9th edition of the *Encyclopaedia Britannica*,[69] which just so happens to be an entry that Lovecraft is known to have copied from directly.[70]

On a sidenote, the etymology of "Qanoon-e-Islam" is interesting. In Mediaeval Arabic, the term *qānūn*—adopted from the Greek κανών—essentially meant 'code of regulations' or 'administrative law' (in a secular sense), as distinct from Islamic law (šarīʿah).[71] In Mediaeval Persian, likewise, the term *qānūn* "came to mean financial and administrative regulations laid down by the ruler independently of the *sharīʿah*."[72] (Indeed, it may come as

---

67 Lovecraft, '*The Case*', in Elliott (com.), *Collected Stories*, I, 73-74.

68 Jaffur Shurreef (trans. Gerhard A. Herklots), *Qanoon-e-Islam, or the Customs of the Moosulmans of India; comprising a full and exact account of their various rites and ceremonies from the moment of birth till the hour of death* (London, UK: Parbury, Allen, and Co., 1832).

69 Edward B. Tylor, 'Magic', in *The Encyclopaedia Britannica: A Dictionary of Arts, Sciences, and General Literature*, 9th ed., complete reprint, vol. 15 (New York, USA: The Henry G. Allen Company, 1890), 203, n. 1.

70 Joshi & Schultz, *An H.P. Lovecraft Encyclopedia*, 115.

71 Yvon Linant de Bellefonds, 'Ḳānūn i.—law', in Emeri J. van Donzel, Bernard Lewis, Charles Pellat, & Clifford E. Bosworth (eds.), *The Encyclopaedia of Islam, New Edition, Volume 4: Iran-Kha* (Leiden, the Netherlands: Koninklijke Brill NV, 1978), 556-557.

72 Said A. Arjomand, 'Constitutions and the Struggle for Political Order: A Study in the Modernization of Political Tradition',

a surprise to those unfamiliar with Islamic history that the šarī'ah was usually applied partially, sporadically, or not at all in pre-modern Muslim societies.[73] Rabbinical law,

---

in Şerif Mardin (ed.), *Cultural Transitions in the Middle East* (Leiden, the Netherlands: E. J. Brill, 1994), 14.

73 E.g., Linant de Bellefonds, 'Ḳānūn i.—law', in Van Donzel *et al.* (eds.), *EI²*, IV, 556, col. 2: "In theory, the *sharī'a* regulates the whole of the public and private life of the Muslim, but since works of *fiḳh* barely deal with the provisions of common law, and also since it became apparent very early on that the greater part of the Muslim penal system was inapplicable, the guardians of public order (especially the governors) took to issuing regulations (*ḳawānīn*) in these two fields, although they had no such legislative authority." Likewise, Ignaz Goldziher & Joseph F. Schacht, '*Fiḳh*', in Lewis *et al.* (eds.), *EI²*, II, 890, col. 2: "For reasons of dynastic policy, and in order to differentiate themselves from their predecessors, the 'Abbāsids posed as the protagonists of Islam, recognized Islamic law as it was being taught by the pious specialists as the only legitimate norm in Islam, and set out to translate their doctrines into practice. [...] But this effort to translate into practice the ideal doctrine which was being elaborated by the specialists, was short-lived. [...] The *ḳāḍīs*, theoretically independent though they were, had to rely on the political authorities for the execution of their judgments, and, being bound by the formal rules of the Islamic law of evidence, their inability to deal

which in certain domains is purely theoretical or ideal, serves as a helpful analogue.) Hence, the Arabic *qānūn al-'islām* and the Persian *qānūn-e 'eslām* both at first glance seem to mean 'the secular laws of Islam', which might seem oxymoronic. However, *qānūn* also came to mean "norm" even in Arabic,[74]

---

with criminal cases became apparent, so that the administration of the greater part of criminal justice was taken over by the police (*shurṭa*). The administrative "investigation of complaints" very soon led to formal Courts of Complaints being set up, which by their very existence show the breakdown of a considerable part of the administration of civil justice by the *ḳāḍīs* as well. In this way, a double administration of justice came into being, and it has prevailed in most Islamic countries, the competence of the *ḳāḍīs*' tribunals being restricted to matters of family law, inheritance, and *waḳf*." For example, concerning the historic non-implementation of stoning for adultery, see Marion Holmes Katz, 'The *Ḥadd* Penalty for *Zinā*: Symbol or Deterrent? Texts from the Early Sixteenth Century', in Paul M. Cobb (ed.), *The Lineaments of Islam: Studies in Honor of Fred McGraw Donner* (Leiden, the Netherlands: Koninklijke Brill NV, 2012), 351-376. For an amusing legal fiction adopted by Mediaeval Muslim jurists to avoid having to punish adulteresses, see Cyril Glassé, *The Concise Encyclopædia of Islam*, 3rd ed. (Walnut Creek, USA: Stacey International, 2008), 496, col. 2.

74 E.g., Wehr (trans. Cowan), *Arabic-English Dictionary*, 863, col. 2.

so there is no necessary contradiction here (whether in Arabic, Persian, or Hindustani): "Qanoon-e-Islam" simply means "the Customs of the Moosulmans", to quote the subtitle given by Herklots.

The rapid spread of Islam

In a 1933 letter to a correspondent named Helen Sully discussing morality and religion, Lovecraft stated the following:

Exceptions to this rule of gradual growth are very rare—coming only when some psychological accident raises up a new illusion so potently captivating that it sweeps all before it. Such an accident was the blazing up of Islam in the 7th Century, and such, to a lesser and perhaps temporary degree, is the spread of communism (a religion despite its anti-theism) in modern Russia.[75]

Lovecraft here expresses a view of the spread of Islam that was common in his era, but which has since been shown to be false: the spread of Islam was in fact quite gradual, whether construed politically (the spread of a Muslim ruling class or a Muslim-dominated state) or religiously (the conversion of populations to Islam).

In the first case (i.e., political spread), it is of course true that the initial Muslim conquests[76] were

of populations to Islam).

In the first case (i.e., political spread), it is of course true that the initial Muslim conquests[76] were

---

75 Lovecraft, 'Religion and Social Progress', in Joshi (ed.), *Against Religion*, 120-121.

76 Actually, even speaking of "Muslim" conquests in the early period poses some problems. In the first place, early Muslims probably did not call themselves 'Muslims' per se: Patricia Crone & Michael A. Cook, *Hagarism: The making of the Islamic world* (Cambridge, UK: Cambridge University Press, 1977), 8-9; Fred M. Donner, *Muhammad and the Believers: At the Origins of Islam* (Cambridge, UK: Harvard University Press, 2010), 57-58, 86, 203; *id.*, 'Robert Hoyland, *In God's Path: The Arab Conquests and the Creation of an Islamic Empire*', al-ʿUṣūr al-Wusṭā, Volume 23 (2015), 137; Ilkka Lindstedt, 'Muhājirūn as a Name for the First/Seventh Century Muslims', *Journal of Near Eastern Studies*, Volume 74, Number 1 (2015), 67-73; Stephen J. Shoemaker, *The Death of a Prophet: The End of Muhammad's Life and the Beginnings of Islam* (Philadelphia, USA: University of Pennsylvania Press, 2012), ch. 4; Ilkka Lindstedt, 'The Makings of Early Islamic Identity', *Freedom to Think! HCAS blog* (9th/October/2019): https://blogs.helsinki.fi/hcasblog/2019/10/09/the-makings-of-early-islamic-identity/; Stephen J. Shoemaker, *A prophet has appeared: The rise of Islam through Christian and Jewish eyes* (Oakland, USA: University of California Press, 2021), 32-34.

More importantly, the early conquest polity was probably a coalition of believers, dominated by proto-Muslims, but also including

rapid: when Muḥammad died in 632 (if we trust the traditional chronology and geography),[77] his

Madinah-based Islamic polity controlled the Hijaz, Yemen, parts of Central Arabia, and Oman; under his political successor ʾAbū Bakr (r. 632-634), the rest of Arabia (up to the edges of Syria-Palestine and Iraq) was added thereto; under ʿUmar (r. 634-644), the nascent empire smashed both the Romans and Persians in open battle, sweeping over Egypt, the Levant, Iraq, and parts of Iran thereafter; and under ʿUṯmān (r. 656-661), the empire further expanded to include the Libyan coasts in the West, Armenia and Azerbaijan in the North, and rest of Iran in the East. This was the period of the Great Conquests: between the death of Muḥammad (632) and the first *fitnah* or Islamic civil war (656-661). By contrast, the later conquests of Central Asia, North Africa, and Spain under the successive Sufyanid and the Marwanid dynasties (both constituting the Umayyad Dynasty overall) dragged on for decades and decades—hardly a *blitzkrieg*.[78]

(unconverted) Jews and perhaps even Christians: Crone & Cook, *Hagarism*, chs. 1-2; Donner, *Muhammad*, 68-75, 96-97; Shoemaker, *The Death of a Prophet*, ch. 4; Hoyland, *In God's Path*, 57-60; Shoemaker, *A prophet has appeared*, 15-23. It was not until the Marwanid period (c. 685-750) that a distinctively and recognisably Islamic identity and state emerged.

77 Cf. Shoemaker, *The Death of a Prophet*, ch. 1. For problems with the chronology of the conquests more broadly, see Patricia Crone, *Slaves on Horses: The Evolution of the Islamic Polity* (Cambridge, UK: Cambridge University Press, 1980), ch. 1; Albrecht Noth & Lawrence I. Conrad (trans. Michael Bonner), *The Early Arabic Historical Tradition: A Source-critical Study*, 2nd ed. (Princeton, USA: The Darwin Press, Inc., 1994); Parvaneh Pourshariati, *Decline and Fall of the*

Sasanian Empire: The Sasanian–Parthian Confederacy and the Arab Conquest of Iran (London, UK: I. B. Tauris & Co. Ltd., 2008), ch. 3.

78 E.g., Ira M. Lapidus, A *History of Islamic Societies*, 3rd ed. (Cambridge, UK: Cambridge University Press, 2014), 46: the conquest of coastal North Africa (i.e., from Libya to the Atlas Mountains) took around seven decades (643-711); the conquest of Spain took around five

Of course, what Lovecraft probably meant was rapid *conversion*, not merely *conquests*—but here too, more recent scholarship has dispelled the popular perceptions of his era. For example, the conversation to Islam of the majority of the population of the Middle East—the *central lands* of the original Arabo-Islamic Empire—may have taken as long as half a millennium.[79] In other words, mass-conversion was extremely rare: for the first few Islamic centuries, Muslims were a tiny minority in their empire, a network of urban colonies in a vast ocean of Christians, Jews, Zoroastrians, Hindus, Buddhists, and others. For decades after the conquests, the administration of the nascent empire remained largely in the hands of a (Christian and Zoroastrian) bureaucracy inherited from the Romans and Persians, and the Sufyanids in particular relied heavily upon the support of Christian Arab tribes in outer Syria, Christian administrators across the Levant and Egypt more broadly, and even Christian soldiers in their armies.[80]

Moreover, under the Marwanids, some efforts were made to prevent or discourage the conquered population from converting to Islam, as a means to protect the imperial tax base (taxation by now having become partially based on religious affiliation).[81]

In short, the early spread of Islam, whether construed in terms of conquest or conversion, was generally more gradual than Lovecraft supposed.

Muḥammad, cats, and dogs

In his 1926 essay 'Cats and Dogs', Lovecraft commented: "I do not wonder that Mahomet, that sheik of perfect manners, loved cats for their urbanity and disliked dogs for their boorishness".[82] The idea that Muḥammad loved cats was—and still is—a popular one, with numerous 19th-Century sources citing the story of the Prophet cutting off his own sleave rather than disturbing a cat sleeping thereon.[83] As such, Lovecraft

---

decades (711-759); and the conquest of Transoxiana was only completed by 751.

79 E.g., Jack Tannous, *The Making of the Medieval Middle East: Religion, Society, and Simple Believers* (Princeton, USA: Princeton University Press, 2018), 340 ff.

80 E.g., Donner, *Muhammad,* 112-115, 176-177, 180-182, 192-193.

81 E.g., Gerald R. Hawting, *The First Dynasty of Islam: The Umayyad Caliphate AD 661-750*, 2nd ed. (London, UK: Routledge, 2000), 77-81.

82 Howard P. Lovecraft, 'Cats and Dogs', in Sunand T. Joshi (ed.), *Miscellaneous Writings* (Sauk City, USA: Arkham House Publishers, 1995), 551.

83 E.g., William B. Daniel, *Supplement to the Rural Sports*

could have obtained this information from anywhere—it was in the literary and popular culture at large, during his era.

This story (not to mention the story that the Prophet had a cat named Muʿizzah) is certainly apocryphal, being absent from any Hadith collection or related source.[84] In fact, it seems to have originated as an anecdote about the Moroccan scholar, ascetic, and saint ʾAḥmad b. ʾabī al-Ḥasan b. Rifāʿah (d. 1182), related as follows in the *Taʾrīḵ al-ʾIslām* of the Syrian Hadith scholar Muḥammad b. ʾAḥmad al-Ḏahabī (d. 1348):

It is said that a cat was sleeping on shaykh ʾAḥmad's sleeve when the time for prayer came, so he cut off his sleeve without disturbing it. When he returned from prayer, he found that [the cat] had arisen, so he stitched the sleeve back on to

his robe and declared: "Nothing has changed!"[85]

Evidently, the story of ʾAḥmad was transferred in popular Muslim imagination back to the Prophet, in a very late example of the process of retrojection that occurred on a wide scale in early Hadith.[86]

---

85 Muḥammad b. ʾAḥmad al-Ḏahabī (ed. ʿUmar ʿAbd al-Salām Tadmurī), *Taʾrīḵ al-ʾIslām wa-Wafayāt al-Mašāhīr wa-al-ʾAʿlām*, vol. 40 (Beirut, Lebanon: Dār al-Kitāb al-ʿArabiyy, 1996), p. 249, # 266.

86 Goldziher (trans. Barber & Stern), *Muslim Studies*, II, 148-149 (incl. n. 3); Joseph F. Schacht, *The Origins of Muhammadan Jurisprudence* (Oxford, UK: Oxford University Press, 1950), *passim*; Michael A. Cook, *Early Muslim Dogma: A Source-critical Study* (Cambridge, UK: Cambridge University Press, 1981), ch. 11; Gautier H. A. Juynboll, *Muslim tradition: Studies in chronology, provenance and authorship of early* ḥadīth (Cambridge, UK: Cambridge University Press, 1983), *passim*; Michael A. Cook, 'Magian Cheese: An Archaic Problem in Islamic Law', *Bulletin of the School of Oriental and African Studies*, Volume 47, Number 3 (1984), *passim*; Patricia Crone, *Roman, provincial and Islamic law: The origins of the Islamic patronate* (Cambridge, UK: Cambridge University Press, 1987), 124, nn. 67-68; Gautier H. A. Juynboll, 'Some notes on Islam's first *fuqahāʾ* distilled from early ḥadīth literature', *Arabica*, Volume 39 (1992), *passim*; Harald Motzki, *Analysing Muslim Traditions: Studies in Legal, Exegetical and* Maghāzī

(London, UK: T. Davison, 1813), 697; Jane Loudon, *Domestic Pets: Their Habits and Management; With Illustrative Anecdotes* (London, UK: Grant & Griffith, 1851), 44-45; 'Something about cats', in *The Boy's Yearly Book: Being the Twelve Numbers of the "Boy's Penny Magazine," (from January to December, 1863)* (London, UK: S. O. Beeton, 1863), 108.

84 Yusuf Shabbir, 'The Prophet's cat Muezza', *Islamic Portal* (9th/ October/2020): https://islamicportal. co.uk/the-prophets-cat-muezza/

Still, Lovecraft's statement about Muḥammad's favouritism towards cats is not completely baseless, at least in terms of the latter's representation in the classical Sunnite Hadith canon: the Prophet reportedly declared that cats are not ritually impure, given their constant close proximity to people in houses.[87] Additionally, it is reported that the Prophet was shown a vision of a woman burning in Hell as punishment for having tied up a cat without feeding it or letting it roam free to catch vermin.[88] However, the first hadith is simply a statement on the purity-related status of cats, and the second can be understood as reflecting a more general condemnation of the mistreatment of animals[89]—neither really imputes a love of cats per se to the Prophet.

There is a stronger case for the Prophet's hostility towards dogs, at least as depicted in the Sunnite canon: the Prophet declared that money earned through a selling a dog is reprehensible,[90] that a vessel from which a dog drinks must be rinsed seven times before it becomes ritually pure,[91] that the presence of a dog breaks a prayer,[92] that angels shun dogs,[93] and that he ordered all dogs to be killed, except for hunting dogs and guard dogs.[94] However, in another hadith, the Prophet abrogates the declaration that the presence of a dog breaks a prayer,[95] and in yet another he moderates the killing order by stating merely that God will lessen the ultimate reward of those who own dogs, except for hunting or guard dogs.[96] (Another hadith likewise assumes the permissibility of hunting dogs.[97]) Finally, the Prophet also told his followers of a man who gave water to a parched dog, for which God rewarded him.[98] In another version of this story relat-

---

Hadīth (Leiden, the Netherlands: Koninklijke Brill NV, 2010), 271; Christopher Melchert, 'Basra and Kufa as the Earliest Centers of Islamic Legal Controversy', in Behnam Sadeghi, Asad Q. Ahmed, Adam Silverstein, & Robert G. Hoyland (eds.), *Islamic Cultures, Islamic Contexts: Essays in Honor of Professor Patricia Crone* (Leiden, the Netherlands: Koninklijke Brill NV, 2015), 178; etc.

87 Gautier H. A. Juynboll, *Encyclopedia of Canonical Ḥadīth* (Leiden, the Netherlands: Koninklijke Brill NV, 2007), 350-351.

88 *Ibid.*, 179, 337.

89 E.g., see *ibid.*, 218.

90 *Ibid.*, 655, 710.

91 *Ibid.*, 362, 532-533.

92 *Ibid.*, 443. Also see *ibid.*, 123.

93 *Ibid.*, 348, 539, 698.

94 *Ibid.*, 170-171, 330, 532-533.

95 *Ibid.*, 548.

96 *Ibid.*, 37, 309-310.

97 *Ibid.*, 138, 411, 418, 687.

98 *Ibid.*, 354-355.

ed from the Prophet, the virtue of helping the dog is even greater: it is a prostitute who gives water to the parched dog, for which her sins are forgiven.[99]

In short, the idea that Muḥammad loved cats is popular one, but one based on extremely late and apocryphal stories: in canonical Hadith at least, he is depicted as merely proclaiming them to be ritually pure, and as condemning their cruel treatment. The idea that he disliked dogs has a stronger basis (given the profusion of anti-dog hadiths in the Sunnite canon), but even then, the picture is not consistent. Certainly, there is no basis for the idea that Muḥammad disliked dogs because of their "boorishness", *pace* Lovecraft. On the contrary, the hostility towards dogs present in Hadith stems from the notion of their ritual impurity, which was inherited from Judaism.[100]

Conclusion

There are numerous literary and historical references to Islam and the Middle East scattered throughout the writings of Lovecraft, some of which play a key rôle in his fictional worldbuilding: no less than the iconic *Necronomicon* is depicted as originating as the work of an Arab poet during the Umayyad period. Lovecraft seems to have primarily drawn upon the *Arabian Nights* and the 9th edition of the *Encyclopaedia Britannica* in this domain, and it comes as no surprise that his writings inherited orientalist attitudes and certain historical misconceptions—both popular and scholarly—that were common in his era. Still, many of Lovecraft's literary and historical references to Islam and the Middle East are apposite or well-applied, lending verisimilitude and depth to his fictional worldbuilding.

---

99 Baššār ʿAwwād Maʿrūf *et al.*, *al-Musnad al-Jāmiʿ*, vol. 17 (Beirut, Lebanon: Dār al-Jīl, 1993), pp. 601-602, # 14178.

---

100 Schacht, *Origins*, 216.

What Would H. P. Lovecraft Have Thought About UFOs?

by Donald R. Burleson

It hardly needs pointing out that the world has changed in countless ways since H. P. Lovecraft's day, but there is one difference about which little has been said—in Lovecraft's time, unidentified flying objects were only rarely, if ever, mentioned, while in our own time they're mentioned quite often.

It isn't as if UFOs were never seen in the 1920s and 1930s. On August 5, 1926, for a notable example, Russian artist and explorer Nicholas Roerich and his climbing party in the Himalayas observed a fast-moving airborne object much too sophisticated in its movements and appearance to be readily explainable in conventional terms at that early stage in the history of aeronautics (Hall, 6). Unfortunately, this sighting incident received little publicity at the time; had it been more widely known, it surely would have captured Lovecraft's interest, given his admiration of Roerich's "weird Thibetan landscapes" if nothing else (Lovecraft, 342).

But the frequency of UFO sightings was not to reach the level of constant press attention until 1947, with the Kenneth Arnold event at Mount Rainier and the Roswell, New Mexico crash episode, in June and July of that year respectively. By then, Lovecraft had been gone for a decade. In any case, one can speculate about how he would have reacted to the whole enigma if he had lived into the 1940s and 1950s and beyond.

His reaction to the UFO question would of course depend on how he learned of the objects. Obviously, the most dramatic way would ideally be to see one himself. It's an unforgettable experience, as I can attest, having had my one and only sighting at the age of five on the night of the Roswell crash in 1947, but three hundred miles east of Roswell, in Breckenridge, Texas, where my family was visiting my grandparents for the July 4th weekend. (Thinking that a little kid could have been mistaken, my wife Mollie and I once visited the site and searched the old newspaper files to find that a number of people had seen and reported the object.)

Given an experience anything like this, Lovecraft, with his penchant for orderly reasoning, would no doubt have spent considerable time puzzling over what he had seen, without necessarily coming to any definite conclusions. But only a small percentage of people

in that time period actually saw UFOs, and had Lovecraft been alive then, he would more likely have learned about the UFO experience in some more vicarious way. (The late physicist Stanton Friedman, renowned UFO researcher, spent his whole life pursuing the subject but never actually saw a UFO himself.)

Most UFO witnesses talk about their sightings to a great many friends, and Lovecraft, if alive when they were happening, might well have heard such an account from someone, in an age when sightings were relatively frequent and much in the news. However, it has always been the case that not all people telling such stories are equally reliable.

Indeed, one hears a great deal of nonsense in this field. If you're a UFO investigator, someone may well tell you that they were abducted, hustled aboard a UFO, and flown to Venus for a personal conference with God. Or someone will tell you, with an air of great authority, that they know exactly where UFOs come from and why they're here—"They come from Zeta Reticulae and they're collecting DNA." Or they will claim to have intimate knowledge of a galactic federation to which humankind belongs though it's known only to government insiders. Sadly, this sort of thing gives the whole field of UFO studies the appearance of being the flying saucer lunatic fringe. Lovecraft would promptly have judged these accounts to be garbage, and he would have been right.

But he might also have heard more sensible sighting accounts from more stable and honest witnesses. Even if one does not have the sighting experience oneself, hearing a solid, sane, level-headed witness breathtakingly tell a story of seeing an anomalous object in the sky can leave one profoundly impressed, though the question of what exactly the object was might remain a matter of conjecture, a process of conjecture in which one may readily imagine Lovecraft indulging with some relish.

Or had he lived a few decades longer, Lovecraft might have read some of the more sensible

and informative books on the subject of UFOs, the literature being quite extensive. But as with witnesses, so with books. They span a broad spectrum from near-idiocy to scientific brilliance. The "hard science" people in the field (I count myself as one) know what Lovecraft also knew—that science is the only trustworthy way to find anything out. Some UFO books (at the idiocy end of the spectrum) were appropriately shelved, in the old walk-in bookstores, alongside books on witchcraft, black magic, and Tarot card reading. Other UFO books, written with integrity, honesty, competence, and a respect for the scientific method, didn't deserve to be shelved with the ludicrous things I mentioned, but were usually shelved there anyway. Lovecraft would have been perfectly capable of discerning the difference, and whatever he chose to read on the topic, he would have drawn his own conclusions, or would have found it appropriate to forgo definite conclusions without more information. His regard for science and logic would have prevailed. He may have come to eschew a personal study of science (as one recalls, he backed away from chemistry at the point where it became mathematical), but he certainly appreciated its illuminative function in the scheme of things.

His view of cosmology may have tended to favor something of a skepticism about things like alien visitors from other worlds, prompting him to seek more conventional explanations for UFOs, had he heard of them. He once remarked, in a letter, that many such science fiction concepts were probably factually wrong: "In the first place, the number of bodies inhabited by highly evolved organic beings at any one period of the cosmos is probably very small" (Lovecraft, 323-4). That is, the likelihood of spontaneous thermo-chemical synthesis of the self-replicating molecules that lead to complex life is (or so some scientists in Lovecraft's day thought) a low probability. In modern times, especially given an enhanced understanding of the age and complexity of the universe, we have revised that probability upwards, but Lovecraft was fairly reflecting the science of his day. (He goes on in the same letter to mention the age of the universe as five billion years, while more recent estimates make it closer to fourteen billion.)

If Lovecraft had lived into the age in which UFO sightings became frequent and more publicized, he might also have taken government pronouncements into account, but here there would have been little to learn. It has only been since mid-2021 that the federal government has even admitted publicly that there are things in our skies that are problematical to identify. This "disclosure" amounts to what many of us call a nothing-burger, though at least they finally acknowledged that such airborne objects exist.

The earlier history of the phenomenon is rife with examples of less honest official pronouncements. They declared the Roswell crash (1947) to be a weather balloon, despite the contrary testimony of hundreds of interviewed witnesses. They declared the Lubbock Lights (1951) to be the reflections of street lamps on high-flying duck bottoms! But I found and interviewed a new witness who saw those eighteen objects from a vantagepoint far out in the country, away from any city lights. So much for illuminated duck butts (Burleson, 43). The authorities declared the Levelland, Texas object that landed in several spots on the roadways (1957) to be "ball lightning." But when I interviewed the daughter of the late sheriff, she said that her father, normally a very robust fellow, was badly frightened by the threatening way in which authorities warned him never to talk about the episode. That seems like a lot of fuss over ball lightning.

Overall, given this history of obfuscation, it seems unlikely that Lovecraft would have found much worth pondering in the statements of the government. As is well known, in his later life he politically abandoned the conservatism of his earlier years and shifted quite a distance to the left. It seems probable, then, that he would have been inclined to regard official statements as having some credibility at least when they were issued by political administrations of a more liberal disposition, but his scientific detachment could have been expected to have the final word, if there can ever be any final word about so open-ended a matter.

In all fairness, although conservatives generally distrust government, many people, not just those on the political left, tend to listen more trustingly to government when it politically aligns more closely with their own proclivities. But the problem in any case with deriving knowledge about the UFO phenomenon is that while government can mostly be counted upon to say nothing important about the question, for most people there is little else to go on. In the field of UFO studies itself, the discourse is rich and informative, but most people rarely if ever see the best of this discourse, having to form their opinions mostly on indirect hearsay from witnesses, should they be exposed to any.

In the end (as if there were any end), UFOs are hard to dismiss honestly. A solid radar track showing an object making a right-angle turn at 5,000 miles per hour is scarcely to be explained as being a wayward crop-duster. But what are these things really?

Lovecraft in our age would no doubt have found himself in the position of having difficulty discovering what there is to be believed. But again, his respect for the thought processes of science would have encouraged him to study carefully whatever information he could find, carefully separated from superstition and folly.

Works Cited

Burleson, Donald R. *The Golden Age of UFOs.* Roswell, NM: Black Mesa Press, 2001.

Hall, Richard H., ed. *The UFO Evidence.* Washington, D.C.: National Investigations Committee on Aerial Phenomena (NICAP), 1964.

Lovecraft, H. P. *Selected Letters 1932-1934* (IV).   August Derleth and James Turner, eds. Sauk City, WI: Arkham House, 1976.

H.P ♡Craft – "Cthylla the Hidden"

HPL—Pioneer Fan

by Will Murray

H.P. Lovecraft was a pioneer in the world of horror fiction. No one could possibly dispute that assertion.

Despite his early Poesque efforts and Dunsanian imitations, Lovecraft lifted himself above the status of semi-amateur dilettante when he penned "The Call of Cthulhu" in 1926 and then built upon the story's theme of "Outsideness" a towering edifice of transcendent horror. Although cosmic horror had existed before, but on a lesser scale, HPL took it literally to the stars.

I need not recapitulate Lovecraft's formidable accomplishments here, in the pages of *Crypt of Cthulhu*. They are well known. But there is another arena where Lovecraft went where no one had gone before, blazing a path and carving out the rudimentary beginnings of his public and professional life. Some of you may be furrowing your brows and scratching your heads. But follow my train of thought....

When I was growing up, before I ever heard of Lovecraft or the Cthulhu Mythos, I read a magazine called *Famous Monsters of Filmland*. It was published to cash in on the monster craze that over-took Hollywood in the 1950s and which spilled over into early television via *Shock Theater* and other ghoul-hosted shows that ran classic horror pictures.

When Publisher James Warren assembled the magazine, he hired as his editor Forrest J Ackerman, a long-time fan and collector. Ackerman's extensive Hollywood contacts and vast collection of movie stills and other memorabilia enabled him to assemble the issues.

No doubt Ackerman is well known to the readers of *Crypt of Cthulhu*. Back in the 1930s, he was notorious for writing to the letter columns of the science fiction and fantasy magazines, where he criticized the appearance of Clark Ashton Smith's "The Dweller on the Martian Gulf" for being too much of a horror story to appear in the pages of *Wonder Stories*. This drew the studied and mocking wrath of Lovecraft and others. HPL noted that "Ackerman once wrote me a letter with a very childish attack on my work...." But Ackerman took it in stride, and went on reading and writing letters for publication. At one point in his fannish life, he counted 127 correspondents. Sound familiar?

Opinionated, eccentric, Forry

read everything he could get his hands on in the field, collected whatever he could, from original art to movie memorabilia, out of which he built a personal and professional life. In his native Los Angeles, he organized SF fandom into a cohesive group, forming lifelong social bonds in fandom.

Ackerman attended the First World Science Fiction Convention in New York in 1939, dressed as a character inspired by the H. G. Well's film, *The Shape of Things to Come*. You could call him a pioneer of cosplay if you wish.

The legendary Ackerman became a literary agent for many science fiction authors of the pulp era, encouraging a young Ray Bradbury, Ray Harryhausen, Charles Beaumont, L. Ron Hubbard, Marion Zimmer Bradley and others, just as HPL did with his acolytes. He also built a virtual museum in his Hollywood home, showcasing the myriad items he collected.

Professionally, Forry didn't break through into the public consciousness until *Famous Monsters of Filmland.* For a long time, he was the premier proponent of science fiction and fantasy, known by various aliases, 4e, 4SJ, the Ackermonster, Dr. Acula and Pharaoh J. Ankh-Er-Man.

He also coined the despised term, "Sci-Fi." In 1953 the World SF Convention gave him an unprecedented Hugo Award which hailed him as "Number 1 Fan Personality." A year later, he acquired the honorary title, "Mr. Science Fiction."

Ackerman is the first person believed to have practiced what science-fiction fandom calls "Fandom as a Way of Life." He lived it, he breathed it, and he graduated from it into the professional realm. But fannish activities dominated his existence from the day he discovered *Amazing Stories* with its first issue in 1926 to his death at the age of 92 in 2008.

Despite his myriad and varied accomplishments, ranging from

some 50 published stories to appearing in several films and documentaries—he never stopped being a fan. It was not in his DNA to do so.

Curious to think that the man who disliked horror fiction so much that he took it upon himself to castigate both the legendary Lovecraft and the immortal Clark Ashton Smith for the audacity to write such material should edit a magazine devoted to monster movies. But Ackerman was a film buff, and he loved horror films.

Of course, there were others who followed in his footsteps. Many of the early science-fiction giants were fans, avid readers, and prolific contributors to the letter-cols. Even within the narrow compass of the 1930s, people like the future creator of Superman, Jerry Siegel, and later *Superman* editors Mort Weisinger and Julie Schwartz, managed to migrate from the mimeographed modesty of the early science-fiction fanzines into editorial positions with SF pulp magazines and their successors, the comic books.

What does this have to do with H.P. Lovecraft, you ask?

Before the rise of Ackerman, the Gentleman from Providence followed a similar trajectory. HPL did not get his start in the science fiction magazines and their associated fandoms, however. He first came out of his social shell when he began writing highly opinionated criticisms to the letter columns of *The Argosy* in 1911. Like Ackerman later, he derided the authors he did not care for, lobbing that they be expelled from the magazine's pages. This frenetic activity brought him to the attention of the president of the United Amateur Press Association, who invited HPL to join in April, 1914. And so Lovecraft began to dabble in amateur journalism, a national circle of aspiring writers that pre-dated science-fiction fandom by two decades or more.

Socially isolated and all but friendless in his Providence neighborhood, the adult Lovecraft commenced contributing to numerous ephemeral publications and swiftly became a rising star who ventured out to attend amateur conventions in Boston, as well as visiting fellow UAPA members in their respective towns. He had found his tribe.

Lovecraft's star might have expired eventually had he remained there. But when *Weird Tales* came into being in 1923, suddenly there was a new focal point for his literary and epistolary endeavors. His amateur activities dwindled thereafter. His interest in horror fiction was in its ascendancy.

New friendships arose, important connections made, and Lovecraft graduated from amateurdom to the beginnings of semi-professional status. It was not a perfect transition, for he never made a consistent living at his writing. But it was a clear continuation of what had commenced in the limited circles of amateur journalism.

If you think about it, the Lovecraft we know today was forged in the crucible of amateur journalism and finished in the **cauldron of** the *Weird Tales* Circle, of which he became the nominal nucleus through the power of his intellect and the force of his personality. Just as Ackerman did later as a literary agent, HPL's encouragement launched dozens of writing careers.

Now to be clear: E'ch-Pi-El and 4SJ were distinctly different fellows. Perhaps it is only that men of a similar eccentric mentality naturally gravitate toward fantasy fiction. Conversely, reading that stuff could have molded their minds along parallel channels. Environment or heredity? Who can say definitively?

Both men were atheists. Both wrote pulp fiction, Ackerman having placed stories here and there between his letter hacking. Lovecraft's literary efforts were seminal, where Ackerman's were ephemeral and often in collaboration with others. He employed more pseudonyms in his professional career than Lovecraft did in his amateur days. Both were fond of puns, although Ackerman to a much greater degree than his older counterpart.

Fandom Is a Way of Life. I daresay Howard Phillips Lovecraft was the first person in American letters to step onto that path. In truth, he blazed it. His star shone more brightly with each transition, including the final one that led to his posthumous fame. And if he never in his lifetime achieved his maximum potential, Lovecraft certainly demonstrated that, had he lived longer, he would have stood out anywhere he went.

If only there had been another mountain for him to climb, or at least a fresh plateau to explore. But life is what it is. And death is its full stop. His time ran out, and in many ways HPL remained a creature of the amateur worlds which spawned him, writing innumerable letters but, sadly, defined by a finite number of classic stories he left to a posterity ever-hungry for more.

Many of us have followed in his pioneering footsteps. I suppose I am one of them. Our numbers are legion, and always growing....

Fun Guys from Yuggoth
The Cryptic Interview: Will Murray

by Darrell Schweitzer

All of the leading Lovecraftian scholars bring some specialty of their own into the field. S.T. Joshi probably knows more philosophy and classical literature than any of us. Robert M. Price knows religion and biblical scholarship. Will Murray's specialty is the pulps. See, for instance, his "Lovecraft and the Pulp Magazine Tradition" in Schultz and Joshi's *An Epicure of the Terrible* (1991), which gives a perspective we don't get from anyone else. That is because, in addition to his scholarly activities, Murray is the leading neo-pulp writer of our time. Had he been born in his grandfather's time, he no doubt would have been a colleague and rival to Lester Dent and Walter Gibson. In our time, he has written authorized Doc Savage novels, not to mention such authorized works as *Tarzan, Conqueror of Mars* and *King Kong vs. Tarzan.* He wrote numerous *Destroyer* novels, which are very much in the tradition of a pulp character series like The Avenger, et al. He has also published a *Mars Attacks* novel and has worked extensively in comics. He even wrote the entire contents of a fake pulp magazine, *Spicy Zeppelin Stories* in 1989.

Q: So, give me some idea of who you are and your background.

Murray: I don't know how to answer that question except to say that I'm a guy who careens from peak experience to peak experience… my latest novel, *Tarzan, Conqueror of Mars,* is my most recent example. In it, the ape-man finally meets John Carter—a solid century after fans first demanded it. The last time I wrote a crossover of such magnitude, Tarzan tangled with King Kong. Don't ask me what's next…I'm running out of peaks….

Q: How did you discover Lovecraft? You are well known as a pulp expert and enthusiast. Did you discover HPL before or after you discovered pulps generally? Did one lead to the other?

Murray: In 1968-69, I started buying paperback books and, completely oblivious to pulp magazines, I somehow gravitated to authors like Edgar Rice Burroughs and Kenneth Robeson, the imaginary author of Doc Savage. I purchased the Lancer Books edition of *The Colour out of Space* in 1969. There wasn't much Lovecraft available in paperback then. Lancer's edition of *The Dunwich Horror* was the only one. This would soon change.

The flood started in 1971 with the Beagle editions and never ceased. I remember Arkham House hardcovers showing up on Paperback Booksmith shelves around that time. I grabbed everything that said Lovecraft on it.

Marvel Comics began adapting Lovecraft late in 1969, but I think I was reading the original stories a few months before that. It was probably HPL's back-cover blurb that prompted me to buy *Zothique* in 1970. I recall vacillating between starting Andre Norton's Witch World series and Conan the Barbarian. Then Marvel announced they were doing Conan. That decided me. Tony Goodstone's *The Pulps* was also published in 1970, so it couldn't have been long before I grasped what pulps were. I recall that in high school I looked up Doc Savage on microfilm in the school library and found the 1966 *Newsweek* article revealing that "Kenneth Robeson" was really Lester Dent. There was a blurry cover of *Doc Savage Magazine* #1 printed therein. That would have been circa 1970 as well.

Q: Did you ever read the bootleg/samizdat novel by S.J. Byrne, TARZAN ON MARS? How bad was it?

Murray: No, I never did. I did read a lengthy review of the story, so I could avoid any inadvertent duplications. My understanding is that it was full of wonderful ideas mixed with occasionally inept execution. Personally, I thought the device of having Jane kidnapped and taken to Barsoom was too much of a cliché. I wanted to write a more compelling story.

I remember reading about his use of the phantom bowman, Kar Komak, and being reminded what a cool character he was. I had forgotten all about him. Too bad he didn't fit my story, I thought. But as my narrative developed, I discovered that he might be useful after all....

Q: Who is publishing your *Tarzan, Conqueror of* Mars?

Murray: Altus Press is publishing it. We've been co-publishers for about nine years now on my books. Beginning with Doc Savage and, as we went along, adding Tarzan, King Kong, the Shadow, the Spider and others, and now reviving John Carter of Mars, who will continue in the Edgar Rice Burroughs' Universe line of books launching in 2020. In the beginning, we had planned only to publish new Doc Savages. But year-by-year it just snowballed until the Wild Adventures series encompassed many major pulp characters and was adopted by Edgar Rice Burroughs, Inc. for their own line of books. None of this was planned. It just happened.

Q: So when you gravitated toward the pulps, at what point were you reading real pulps, not just paperback reprints of them? How do you think that changed your perspective?

Murray: I think I started buying

pulp magazines circa 1973. Initially, I just wanted to read the Doc Savage stories Bantam Books had yet to reprint, supplemented by whatever Shadow magazines I could afford. I guess I just love the pulp magazine format, awkward as it was. They were the same stories, but they had a different feeling in magazine form, like a cross between a comic book and a paperback with old-fashioned illustrations. I loved the covers, the editorials, and everything about them—except their brittleness.

Q: How did you get the Burroughs estate to go along? They have a long history of stoutly resisting pastiches by others, as in their suppression of the Barton Werper Tarzans and the Byrne *Tarzan on Mars*.

Murray: Essentially the same way I got the rights to King Kong: Through my cover artist, Joe DeVito. Joe is connected to the estate of Merian C. Cooper, King Kong's creator. Through Joe, we got permission to pit Doc Savage against King Kong in *Skull Island*. Set just after World War I, it was something of a Burroughsian narrative. Around that time, two people who were Burroughs fans separately suggested I approach Edgar Rice Burroughs, Inc., to see about doing Tarzan. As it happened, Joe had worked with the company, sculpting the Tarzan centennial statue and other projects. So he reached out to them on my behalf, and the ball started rolling.

I'm only guessing here, but I think they were opening up to the idea of new Tarzan novels and I just happened to be the first person who inquired who possessed appropriate credentials. If you can write vintage Doc Savage successfully, Tarzan might be in your wheelhouse, too. About a year after I did *Tarzan: Return to Pa-uldon*, we started talking about *King Kong vs. Tarzan,* which is one of my more successful novels. I've been very lucky. But some of that luck was thanks to Joe DeVito.

Q: But we are supposed to be talking about Lovecraft here. How do you see Lovecraft in a pulp context? It is clear that, after an early immersion in the Munsey magazines, he spent the rest of his life trying to get the pulp cooties out of his prose. Was he perhaps mistaken in this? Could he have gained something positive from the pulps?

Murray: Years ago, I researched an article on Lovecraft, the thesis being that he wasn't really a pulp writer. He just happened to be published in pulp magazines. The more I delved into the subject, the more I came to realize my thesis was upside down. Lovecraft was a pulp guy, plain and simple. But he stood head and shoulders above most so-called "pulpsters."

I wish to God he had created a pseudonym for lesser stories instead of ghosting for people whose drivel wasn't worth ghosting. We could today have an entire separate body of work that, although it might have been second-tier, would have meant probably another volume of Lovecraft stories. Like many creative people, H. P. L. was his own worst enemy.

Q: Do you really think Lovecraft would have written "lesser" stories for the pulps under a pseudonym? That sort of deliberate commercialism seems utterly unlike him. I think he was able to write without total sincerity (or even resort to parody) in his revision work because he did not regard it as real writing.

Murray: Lovecraft was perfectly capable of writing the kind of short filler stories that he once turned out in numbers. Unambitious Poe-esque stuff like "In the Vault" and "Cool Air." He thought he had outgrown such minor tales, but I think he could have turned them out in sufficient numbers to keep himself more financially stable. Assuming, of course, that Farnsworth Wright would have accepted the bulk of them. Not a safe bet. The pseudonym would be optional, of course.

Q: I remember that you wrote an article suggesting that HPL *did* attempt to tailor "The Shadow over Innsmouth" to *Strange Tales* with the long chase sequence. So, would he compromise himself in order to make a sale?

Murray: There are any number of Lovecraftian complaints in his letters to the effect that his prior attempts to hew toward editorial demands had damaged his ability to write on the literary level to which he aspired. Clearly, he made these attempts, and not just with "Innsmouth." *At the Mountains of Madness* was artificially contrived to be divided into a two-part *Weird Tales* novelette. But it didn't work with Wright, alas. And he was able to whip out the humorous answer story, "The Haunter of the Dark" without any inhibition. And what is "Herbert West—Reanimator" except a base pandering to a cheap market? Any story he finished was certain to be published—eventually. I sometimes think that Lovecraft derived the wrong lessons from both his successes and failures.

Q: Considering your own very different approach to writing (I am looking at your bibliography on the Internet SF Database—all those Destroyer novels) how do you think you and Lovecraft would have gotten along if you'd been contemporaries? Would you have made an argument with him that pulp writing can be "art" too?

Murray: I once read an account where Lovecraft dawdled in a stationary store for three hours, painstakingly selecting a fountain pen, while his out-of-town visitors milled helplessly around him. If he had done that to me, my patience would have been worn thin damn quick. I have met persons with some of HPL's personality quirks, and they invariably irk me. But I am also a patient soul. So who knows?

From the standpoint of 1933, the only argument one could make is that if you can sell a certain number of throwaway stories to finance more ambitious tales, the trade-off works, especially since HPL started popping up in anthologies, offering secondary sales. From the standpoint of the 21st-century, I would say, "Write while you can. Your time is short." But I don't get to make either argument, do I?

Q: The pen episode seems a bit out of character for Lovecraft, who was always courteous to his guests, but he could be impulsive at times, too. I recall the account in Cook's memoir of how HPL sat up all night with a cat asleep in his lap and didn't get any writing done, because he didn't want to disturb kitty. (I can't help but think, indelicately, perhaps as an indication of my own age, that if he really did sit there all night, he must have had amazing bladder control.)

But I also remember that he remarked that when writing the "Herbert West" stories he had "become a grub street hack," and that the material was too degraded for amateur publication, although perhaps some of the ideas might be reworked for amateur use later. His anti-professional stance must have been more than an affectation, don't you think? I know an illustrator who says he only accepts select assignments because if the illustration calls for "a Chinaman on a bicycle with a spaceship in the background," he just is not interested in drawing that, much less doing it over and over again. HPL must have been like that. In his own work he seems to have been writing purely to gratify himself. He did "hack" work in his revisions only, or in special cases like the *Home Brew* stories. But is there any real distinction between "professional" work well done and "artistic" writing?

Murray: If there is, I wouldn't know how to codify it.

Q: Is there any evidence that HPL kept up with the pulps after he swore off reading them sometime in the 'Teens? We know he read *Weird Tales*, and he bought the first couple years of *Amazing* for the reprints, but I can't think of much else. Is there any indication that he still indulged in his old, secret vice?

Murray: If mature Lovecraft occasionally read the odd pulp, there exists scant evidence. I believe from his letters that he sampled stuff like *Dime Mystery Magazine* and *Terror Tales* in order to ascertain its availability as a market for his own work. He was profoundly disappointed. He probably did the same thing when they revived *Ghost Stories* in pulp format.

I do recall him mentioning seeing the first issue of *Nick Carter Magazine*, when the old dime novel hero was revived in his own pulp magazine. I doubt that he purchased it. But I would like to think that he sampled *The Shadow* early on, since the radio show was giving the nation the shivers in 1930-31. I recently read that Dashiell Hammett was a regular reader of *Doc Savage Magazine*, so one never knows what an author's secret vices might have been.

Q: My own guess is that HPL did not read many pulps later in life. Maybe he read an *Astounding* or two if it contained a story by one of his friends. But he seems to have felt a sense of guilt about immersing himself in them and feared that this had wrecked his chances of becoming a "real writer" like Blackwood or Dunsany. Would you agree? Was he right?

Murray: I'm not certain of the answer here. Lovecraft loved fantastic fiction so much I would think any reading restraint he showed had more to do with the cost of a pulp magazine than any other factors. I suspect that he read selected issues of *Argosy* whenever a fantastic serial was running. Of course, a lot of the early science-fiction pulp stories were crude and clumsily written, having absolutely no aesthetic impact. I don't think reading pulp fiction would have limited HPL's artistic growth. Many pulp writers got their start by reading magazine stories they thought were so bad they could do better. And so they were inspired to write fiction and became major contributors. A badly-executed story with a great central idea can be as inspirational as a classic. Case in point: HPL was motivated to pen "The Haunter of the Dark" in response to Robert Bloch's "The Shambler from the Stars."

Along that line, I have an article coming up in Centipede Press's *Weird Fiction Review* where I delve into the evidence suggesting that nothing less than *At the Mountains of Madness* was triggered by a failed H. Warner Munn sequel to Poe's *Arthur Gordon Pym.* With Munn's blessing, Lovecraft wrote his own version. And wasn't "The Shadow out of Time" also a response to something HPL read?

I feel that Lovecraft's expressed opinions were often at odds with his own efforts—or at least rationalized responses to past failures. But Lovecraft's case was almost unique in that he was unbending in his own views of what a good story should be and what people should be reading. With his self-defeating attitudes, it was fortunate for him that he didn't end up homeless.

Q: So, what are you mostly writing these days?

Murray: Presently, I have just released my authorized novel, *Tarzan, Conqueror of Mars.* This marks the first time Tarzan of the Apes and John Carter meet, at least in the context of traditional Edgar Rice Burroughs continuity. The premise is simple: Tarzan finds himself marooned on Mars and must find a way home. But first he has to figure out strategies for survival on a dying planet where hardly any forests or game such as he knows them exist.

I'm immensely proud of being allowed to write this book. Burroughs fans have probably been asking for a novel like this for a century—certainly since the 1920s. My *King Kong vs. Tarzan* novel was extremely well received, as was *Skull Island,* wherein Doc Savage encountered Kong. Those were all milestone crossovers for the characters involved, as well as for Will Murray. I think the only thing left to do in that department is to have Doc Savage tangle with Tarzan.

In between chapters, I've been writing Sherlock Holmes stories for the MX and Belanger Books anthologies. I think I've written close to 20 of these by now. In one of them, the Great Detective shares an adventure with Algernon Blackwood's John Silence.

Q: You are doing a lot with other people's characters. You have probably done more of this sort of thing with pulp characters than anybody this side of Philip Jose Farmer. I am sure that is great fun, but do you feel the urge to launch some major work or series that is entirely your own?

Murray: I suspect that I may hold the record outside of comic books for a writer playing with other people's property. But less and less, I think about doing a character of my own. In the last decade, I have revived Doc Savage, The Shadow, Tarzan of the Apes, John Carter of Mars, King Kong, The Spider and a few others. These are beloved characters, and among my favorites. And there's something about stepping into another author's shoes and trying to write in their style that appeals to me. I often say I'm writing the dream stories I wish someone else had written decades ago for me to enjoy.

I think the only thing I've written in recent years that could be called my own, would be my e-book, *Forever After*, which is the story of the day God woke up and couldn't remember who he was. Even there, I'm not sure I can take full credit for it. It's a channeled work. I had no idea what it was about, or where it was going, all the way through to the final chapter.

I do have a few ideas for novels, but I also have contracts for other revivals, such as my new series featuring the semi-insane pulp hero, The Spider.

Characters I created for others, such as Marvel's Squirrel Girl, and the children of Remo Williams in The Destroyer books, have gone on to have a life of their own without me. Given what a superhero icon Squirrel Girl has become, I imagine that despite some 75 published novels, my obituary will begin: CREATOR OF SQUIRREL GIRL DIES.

Q: Do you feel that Lovecraft has had any lasting influence on your own writing?

Murray: Other than writing the occasional Cthulhu Mythos story, I don't think Lovecraft has had a significant influence on my writing. I write heroic fiction, and Lovecraft was a profoundly anti-heroic writer. But I love his work.

I did introduce a kind of restrained version of Cthulhu in one of my Destroyer novels, *Coin of the Realm*. A Kraken-like octopus-god called Sa Mangsang, the Dream Thing. It was meant to be a one-shot, but to my horror, subsequent Destroyer scribes have run with him. And apparently run him into ground....

Q: Turning to your non-fiction, I read your article about Charles Fort in *The PS Book of Fantastic Fiction-eers*, to which we both contributed. What about the connection between Charles Fort and Lovecraft? I doubt Fort read Lovecraft, but it is clear that Lovecraft read Fort. Somewhere in his letters Lovecraft says that he cannot take Fort seriously as science, but he can see how Fort's books could inspire fantastic fiction. Do you see a direct link there? Did HPL take up his own advice?

Murray: The only association

I ever made between Lovecraft's stories and Charles Fort's books is the mention of the fallen meteor "drawing the lighting" in "The Color out of Space." In *The Book of the Damned,* Fort writes about early erroneous dismissals of meteorites as mere terrestrial stones that had been struck by lightning, thereby explaining away the curious fact that they were hot. They were dubbed thunder stones or lightning stones, and were assumed to possess lightning-attracting properties. For decades, scientists flatly dismissed the idea of meteors falling from the sky, amazingly enough.

Q: HPL was a skeptic, but Fort in his own way was, too. Do you see similarities between the two?

Murray: Well, they were both iconoclastic in their way. And nihilistic in their views of life. Each man possessed a self-deprecating sense of humor about life, although Lovecraft plainly worshipped science while Fort took a skeptical view of scientists. Come to think of it, Lovecraft did as well, but only in his fiction. His learned men were continually blundering into the unknown and being psychologically defenestrated by it. So maybe they were closer in temperament than I imagined.

It's almost forgotten now, but Fort wrote for the early pulp magazines. Most of his fiction was pedestrian, but there are several works which have not survived, and which are apparently extreme science fiction, although it's not clear if they were actually fiction or provocative thought experiments. One was titled *X*, and theorized that intelligent beings on Mars were secretly manipulating Earthly events. Another, *Y*, concerned a malign Antarctic civilization. Here, the two writers shared an interest in the then little-explored South Pole. Wouldn't it be amusing if they had mined similar territory? As contemporaries, they might well have embraced parallel concepts.

Fort's idea that we are property is analogous with the Lovecraftian view of mankind as insignificant beings against the cosmic magnitude of the Great Old Ones. Both men lived bookish, intellectual lives and both were fascinated by the bizarre.

Q: Regarding your various articles, I have certainly read the ones in various magazines and anthologies about HPL and the pulps. You don't seem to be that much preoccupied with theory. I can't imagine you doing Deconstruction. What do you think is the most interesting thing you have brought out in your non-fiction?

Murray: Well, I'm interested in exploring the origins of writers' ideas and how they execute those inspirations. Literary theory is not for me. It's too speculative. Not that I haven't written speculative articles. I think it was Dave Schultz who referred to some of my work for *Crypt of Cthulhu* as glorified footnotes or some such terminology.

I wrote dozens of articles for *Crypt* that were just for fun. When the zine was coming out eight times a year, Bob Price needed a lot of material and both he and I would grab at every opportunity to fill pages and enlighten and amuse *Cryptic* readers. I believe I coined the term "The Clark Ashton Smythos."

My most serious articles usually appeared elsewhere. "The Dunwich Chimera and Others" ran in *Lovecraft Studies*. It was an evolution of a college paper I did when I noticed the Greek myths were often perverted or inverted for some Mythos stories. The line, "The Old Ones were, the Old Ones are, and the Old Ones shall be" is clearly derived from the chant, "Zeus was. Zeus is. Zeus will be." And Wilbur Whateley from "The Dunwich Horror" is nothing less than a modern Chimera. Other examples exist, including entries in Lovecraft's Commonplace Book, where he specifically writes about wanting to adapt the Greek myth of Trophonius for a horror story.

I recall once thinking, "Well, that's my only contribution to the understanding of H. P. Lovecraft." It was originally accepted by *Nyctalops*, which went on hiatus. Subsequently, with the advent of Cryptic Publications and Necronomicon Press, I went on to write literally scores of articles for *Lovecraft Studies*, *Nyctalops*, *Dagon*, *Studies in Weird Fiction*, *Fangoria*, and many others. As was the case with the original *Weird Tales* Circle, all this sub-literary industry was the result of friendships that formed in Lovecraft fandom during the 1980s.

Then there was "H. P. Lovecraft and the Pulp Tradition." I actually started a draft of that based on the prevailing idea that Lovecraft spurned the pulp magazines. Then certain clues in the *Selected Letters* made me dig deeper, ultimately forcing me to throw out that draft and start anew. My conclusion was that Lovecraft was a "pulp-hound," to use his own derogatory term, and so tried to crash any number of pulp magazines, including writing an action scene into "*The Shad-*

ow over Innsmouth" in hopes of making *Strange Tales*. It was only his repeated failures to do so that caused him to denigrate these magazines. The enthusiastic contributor to early 1920s *Weird Tales* and the disheartened HPL of the 1930s were almost two different men.

My "In Search of Arkham Country" article looking into the factual origins of Miskatonic locales I think is also important, but my findings have become distorted by confusions over what I actually wrote, owing to an error I made in a follow-up article for the Lovecraft Centennial Conference nearly thirty years ago, where I inadvertently contradicted myself.

My discovery that HPL helped E. Hoffmann Price write his 1934 *Weird Tales* story, "Tarbis of the Lake," is noteworthy—even if the semi-collaboration is not intensely Lovecraftian.

Lastly, my interview with Harry K. Brobst on his memories of Lovecraft was important enough to be reprinted by Arkham House.

Q: Then there is your short Lovecraftian fiction to be considered. You've certainly been a reliable contributor to my anthologies. Will we one day see a book of your Lovecraftian fiction?

Murray: Actually, I've been talking to my publisher, Matt Moring of Altus Press, about collecting some of my twenty-odd Lovecraftian stories. I think I've written nine or ten involving the X-files-ish government organization, the Cryptic Events Evaluation Task Force. So this might be coming out one of these years. I will have to be careful assembling it, though. Someone once pointed out that many of my stories culminate in the destruction of the Earth, mankind or the universe. That would make for a rather depressing collection.…

Q: I had a similar problem when gathering stories for *Cthulhu's Reign*. They can't all end "and then everybody died hideously." That would be monotonous, to say the least. So how do you plan to get around it? A careful arrangement of the stories for maximum contrast is one thing you can do. Another is to deliberately write a couple stories for the collection (even if they are published elsewhere first) which vary from the others as much as possible.

Murray: I plan on bookending the collection with a pair of stories that mirror one another, "To Clear the Earth" and "Black Fire." They concern artifacts planted at either Pole, which are intended to activate when

the stars are right and begin the process of cleansing the planet's surface of mankind. While disaster is averted on one Pole in both tales, the threat on the opposite Pole remains, biding its time....

One sequence of end-of-world stories forms a quadrilogy, so I will probably run those consecutively. And I know I've written at least two humorous stories. So we do have variety of theme and tone. I should be able to make it work.

Q: Finally, what about the Friends of HPL and the plaque at the Centennial Conference? What was your involvement in that?

Murray: I wrote about this in a Necronomicon Press booklet. In the run-up to the Lovecraft Centennial of 1990, S.T. Joshi and I came into contact with a young Lovecraftian, Jon Cooke. Jon had the audacious idea of having the city of Providence erect a statue or some similar monument to the Old Gent in time for the Centennial conference. Unfortunately, the conference was at the time only fourteen weeks away. Nevertheless, we three sat around my dining room table and brainstormed something that against all odds worked out. We formed the Friends of H.P. Lovecraft, and fundraised furiously to place a memorial plaque on the grounds of the John Hay Library. Not only did our fellow Lovecraftians donate generously to this preposterous scheme, but we succeeded in having the plaque dedicated on the last day of the Centennial. Hard to believe that this was almost thirty years ago now. That may be my finest Lovecraftian hour, although I can't say that I was the prime mover. But I did my share.

Q: Thanks, Will.

Robert M. Price

Fun Guys from Yuggoth
The Cryptic Interview: David E. Schultz

by Darrell Schweitzer

Lovecraftians will notice David E. Schultz's name on quite a lot of books on their shelves, usually sharing a byline with S. T. Joshi, everything from *Epicure of the Terrible* (1991) through the recent volumes of Lovecraft's various correspondences. He doesn't seem to get as much attention as some other people in the field. Is he the "silent Lovecraftian?"

Q: So, tell me something of your background, who you are, where you were educated, and of course how you discovered Lovecraft.

Schultz: I'm a native Milwaukeean and have lived here all my life. I'm currently "retired" after spending 26 years (plus 5) as a technical editor in the publications department of CH2M HILL, an engineering company. I graduated from Marquette University with an English degree—the sort of education endlessly lampooned on *A Prairie Home Companion.*

When I was in grade school, I was becoming interested in science fiction, thanks to finding *Fahrenheit 451* and *The Martian Chronicles* in what I think were monthly book order forms the teachers used to distribute. When I was in high school, I haunted the book racks in whatever store had them. Department stores, the grocery, anything. Once when I was with my parents at a Treasure Island store, as they did their business, I was examining the racks. I came upon a provocatively titled and covered book, by a writer I never heard of. The name "H. P. Lovecraft" was, to me, unusual but compelling. The book was *The Colour out of Space* (Lancer, 1964). The cover, depicting a skull on a black background, with flames crackling in the foreground, attracted me (even though it has absolutely nothing to do with the contents), along with the declaration that Lovecraft was "The great modern master of supernatural terror." So I bought it. "The Picture in the House," "Cool Air," and "The Terrible Old Man" were satisfying. The author clearly was more "literary" than most of the science fiction writers I had been reading, and I liked that. "The Call of Cthulhu" (what on earth could that be?) and "The Colour out of Space" were knockout stories, to me, with the opening line of the former and the concluding line of the latter. "The Whisperer in Darkness" and "The Shadow Oout of Time" were a bit beyond me, and it took some time before I could enjoy them.

At around the same time, I came upon Bradbury's story "Pillar of Fire," in *A Treasury of Great Science Fiction* (1959), the come-on to joining the Science Fiction Book Club—two fat volumes for a dime! In it, Bradbury ticked off all the writers whose books were banned in the future. Poe and Lovecraft, but also Machen and Derleth and Bierce (who?). Well, since they were taboo, I just had to look them up. I noticed that the copyright page in *The Colour out of Space* acknowledged permission to include the stories as granted by Arkham House, Sauk City, Wisconsin. Wisconsin? I *live* there! So I asked Mrs. Connelly, the librarian at Marquette University High School, if she could look up the address. She did. I requested a catalogue, and promptly ordered the three books of Lovecraft's fiction and his *Collected Poems* (with *Fungi from Yu-*

ggoth). These strange books provoked strange questions from those who saw them. My high school English teacher thought they must be sex books (because of the author's name). My father saw reference to *Marginalia* in the jacket copy of a book and asked, "What is that? Some kind of *pornography*?" I nevertheless devoured the books, though I was not particularly keen on *The Dream-Quest of Unknown Kadath* and similar stories. And before long, I ordered the first volume of *Selected Letters.* The others had not yet been published.

Somehow I got Meade Frierson's *HPL,* and soon learned about other fanzines devoted to Lovecraft and similar writers. I had no idea there was such an underground publishing network.

Q: So, when did you realize that Lovecraft was a writer to be studied, not just read? Ray Bradbury is a substantial author, for instance, but I do not see you attempting Bradbury scholarship. Or did you at the time?

Schultz: Bradbury was a living author, still producing. Still an open book, as it were. Although Bradbury was a very good writer, I found Lovecraft to be somewhat "literary" (but also pulpy), and aligned somewhat with my reading in college. In fact I believe I wrote a paper or two on Lovecraft when I was in college. I spent a lot of time in the stacks at the Marquette library, noting the myriad books *about* writers. For example, William Faulkner's *The Sound and the Fury* was not an easy book for me to grasp on first reading, and so I found some books that helped me to navigate it. I saw how critics or scholars approached and dealt with their subjects. That's part of my initiation. In the early '70s, not much was available on Lovecraft at all, much less "scholarly" or critical stuff. What was available was . . . well, *fannish.* Pretty weak stuff, but that was all that was available, so I eagerly absorbed the fan publications—not many, but *Nyctalops* was a must-have—hoping there would be something genuinely interesting or informative. At the same time, the Beagle edition of Lovecraft was appearing. And so in 1972, the appearance of Lin Carter's *A Look behind the Cthulhu Mythos* seemed to offer some writing about Lovecraft and his work. Well, it wasn't a very satisfying book. In 1973 I joined the Esoteric Order of Dagon Amateur Press Association. I had no idea what to contribute, and so submitted a long poem. Not very good. But I stuck with that for a while. I heard from the MinnCon group in Minneapolis around that time and soon was driving to Minneapolis to meet with Jack Koblas and Eric Carlson (editors of *Etchings and Odysseys*), Richard L. Tierney, Joseph A. West,

et al. At the first gathering I attended, I met Lovecraft researcher R. Alain Everts. He soon was conducting his own MadCons in Madison, and he started the Necronomicon Amateur Press Association, which was meant to circulate scholarly content. I also met Kenneth W. Faig, Jr., Dirk W. Mosig, and George T. Wetzel. They also belonged to the EOD.

I mostly hung in the shadows, listening to them talk about Lovecraft. They knew much, much more than what I was reading in the fanzines and available books. Of course, most of what they said went straight over my head. They would discuss a mysterious figure named *Barlow* in a very knowing way.

It fascinated me that there was so much that could be known about Lovecraft, even though the information be concentrated in these three individuals. (And how did I happen to stumble into their combined company?) I think the single thing that affected me most, that showed me one could seriously study the life and work of H. P. Lovecraft, was a monograph by

Ken Faig that he called *Lovecraftian Voyages.* What a wealth of information! I had no idea. Ken was, and still is, light years ahead of me in terms of discoveries about Lovecraft. When I learn something that I think is new, I find that Ken had already left footprints in that territory.

I felt a little out of my element in the "scholarly" apa. [Amateur Press Association. – DS] What would I contribute? I didn't know anything that everyone else did not already know. At the time, I had been reading Lovecraft's *Selected Letters,* of which only 3 volumes were available at the time. I also was reading Willis Conover's *Lovecraft at Last* and L. Sprague de Camp's biography of Lovecraft. It occurred to me that the chronological list of Lovecraft's fiction in *Dagon* was incredibly inaccurate, because Lovecraft's letters, and the handy list in Conover's book, in Lovecraft's handwriting, indicated that. Knowing the order in which the stories were written would be insightful to those studying his work (including me). And so I scoured the scant publications available to determine what I could about when the stories were written, and my first contribution to the Necronomicon apa was a revised chronology. The final two volumes of *Selected Letters* would not be published for several years, but Lovecraft's handwritten chronology sufficed for guidance, since in his later years, he wrote only one story per year, more or less.

In the mid-1970s, Everts's Strange Company was planning to publish Lovecraft's *Commonplace Book,* as compiled by Ken Faig. I'd never heard of such a thing. A "commonplace book"? Everts distributed proofs among the group, which we were to return with corrections. How anyone could proofread such a thing cold, without something to consult, was beyond me. And so, I didn't turn in any corrections, but I was grateful for the opportunity to read the book. I still have the proofs of the stillborn book. Ken did not undertake annotation of the entries, but he did write a long introduction about the book. At around this time, Everts gave me a copy of *The Shuttered Room,* which contained the commonplace book. With light annotation, mostly indicating which entries Derleth used to write his so-called posthumous collaborations with Lovecraft. I thought to myself, heck, I can identify which of these Lovecraft used in writing stories and poems, and so one of my early projects was to make my own edition of Lovecraft's commonplace book. Ultimately I ran a sizeable zine through the EOD with all the entries and all my annotations.

But before I got very far with all that, I undertook my study of Lovecraft's *Fungi from Yuggoth.* I ran a number of submissions through the Necronomicon, again annotating the text, writing up a detailed bibliography, and composing an essay about its composition. (Mind you, that work begun c. 1975 did not come to fruition as a book until 2017.)

Q: What was the impact of Lovecraft fandom on you, in the beginning?

Schultz: Fandom was energizing. It probably didn't even really matter that the focus was a writer named H. P. Lovecraft. My feeling was that I was part of a group of detectives, sifting through clues, looking for information. Also, the avenues for conversation—the MinnCons and MadCons—were important. Oh, there was the usual fannish silliness at those things. But there was also much more. I had absolutely nothing to offer, since I was still learning the ropes. I don't consider Everts, Faig, and Mosig to be "fans" in the usual sense of the word. Heck, I don't consider myself a fan—a fanatic. I'm no fanatic about Lovecraft. No, they were a cut above in terms of their knowledge and their prowess at research, and I admired them.

My own early projects were done with something of a fan mentality, but when life intervened—a job, a family, etc.—Lovecraft somewhat dropped into the background. I'd still read and research, but not vigorously. And I think that over time I lost interest in pure fandom, and maybe gafiated for a time. I don't think I'm being a snob, I just don't get worked up by tentacles and prayer breakfasts. But those early years laid the groundwork for my later books, not only with respect to Lovecraft.

Robert Bloch once said "Lovecraft was my university." Now, I don't adore Lovecraft, and I'm not an adherent or anything. But I feel the same sentiment. In that single person was a tremendous wealth of knowledge on many, many subjects, and as I continue to work on books about him, I still learn from what seems to be a bottomless spring of knowledge.

Q: I gather that you have little time for the more frivolous side of Lovecraft studies. No need for prayer breakfasts and the like if you don't want to, but what did you think of Peter Cannon's *Scream for Jeeves*? Do you sometimes see an undercurrent of humor in Lovecraft and even Lovecraft studies? I confess I was warped early by an encounter with Ron Goulart's "Ralph Walstonecraft Hedge: A Memoir," which is a parody of a typical Arkham House Lovecraft memoir.

Schultz: Yes, I don't relish the constant joking about Lovecraft and his work. I'll admit that when a certain publisher once parodied Necronomicon Press's Lovecraft journal as *Lovecraft Stuffies,* I was a little miffed. It seemed to imply that *Lovecraft Studies* was just a little too uptight or something, but I suppose it was meant to be good clean fun. The Cthulhu plushy dolls sadden me. But I suppose that any historic personage is inevitably going to be lampooned. Look at the Abraham Lincoln figure with the undignified opening and closing legs as an obstacle at the miniature golf course on *The Simpsons.* But the writers weren't lampooning Lincoln, only the way we in the 20th century exploit things that ought not to be exploited.

I was at a NecronomiCon (back in the 1990s). At the hotel, I was steered to one of the conference rooms where we were to meet Peter. In the front of one room, a fellow was reading aloud a story. We had walked in in the middle so I didn't know who it was or what was being read. We sat and listened. And it was pretty funny. I recognized the parody of Lovecraftian tropes. And also some Sherlock Holmes. A third element was unknown to me at the time, and that was P. G. Wodehouse. And so I learned that was Peter. Now, reading *about* the nature of his work on paper—his *oeuvre,* if you will—I'd probably have dismissed the concept as a very far-out exercise. How could a Lovecraft–Holmes–Wodehouse (whoever *he* was) mashup even work, much less be funny? Well, seeing—uh, hearing—is believing. First thing I did when I got home was obtain a volume of the collected Jeeves and Bertie stories. I have Peter to thank for introducing me to Wodehouse. I now have nearly all the Overlook Press edi-

tions. Also, I got a kick out of the work of Mortimer Morbius Moamrath, who wrote for *Weird Trails,* edited by Durango Fear, "The Riders of the Purple Ooze." The brainchild of Joe Pumilia and Bill Wallace.

I am beginning to see that Lovecraft himself—despite his dictum that the weird tale not have humor in it—is virtually always doing shtick. Mind you, it's not usually the broad, obvious sort of humor, although "The Hound," "Herbert West—Reanimator," and "The Loved Dead" make me a liar. Steve Mariconda points out that Lovecraft is nearly always *playing,* and I see that manifestly in his letters, of course, but I'm told that can also be found in his fiction. He makes little in-jokes that sometimes only he himself can get. There's a well-known cartoon in the *Zenith,* an amateur journal, with caricatures of many of Lovecraft's associates. The caricature of him shows a dour, scowling Lovecraft with the caption "Lovecraft laughing." So it seems that his colleagues thought him to be humorless at best, perhaps even anti-humor. And yet the evidence in his writings suggests otherwise. Of course his humor is more subtle and involves wordplay. Just look at the salutations in his letters to James F. Morton.

Just this week I stumbled upon a late letter mentioning the birth of kittens in his neighborhood "at the trans-hortensic taberna I chronicled in mid-February." Now, he uses the same phraseology in at least four letters, but only recently did I try to figure out what the phrase meant. Trans = across, of course. Hortense = garden. And taburna = a shop in ancient Rome, or a tavern in Spain. Across the rear garden at 66 College was the Arsdale, a boardinghouse. I'm not entirely sure how the boardinghouse can be considered a shop or tavern, but his aunt did take meals there. In any case, there's also his usual polysyllabic way of referring to something commonplace, such as "saline ocular effusions" for tears. The notion that Lovecraft would weep regarding some sad matter is comic enough, but his verbal description sends it over the top. Whether those reading about the taberna had any idea what he meant, I don't know. They may have been able to deduce it somewhat from recalling the mention in a previous letter about the cats and their birthplace. When Lovecraft's aunt was hospitalized in 1936, he wrote a daily diary to apprise her of his activities. One day he wrote "Retired 5:30 a.m. after a bit of Sam Singing." I beg your pardon? What on earth could that possibly mean? Clearly his aunt would understand, and possibly chuckle at the way Lovecraft phrased it. What he meant was he had done some laundry. He alludes to the nearby Sam Sing Laundry, which closed only in 2002. The point is, even if Lovecraft's quips didn't amuse anyone else, they amused him.

Few recognize this aspect of Lovecraft, and the only humor seen in Lovecraft is what one finds on the covers of his books. Book covers equate things Lovecraftian with *tentacles.* And in comic form at that. I don't see it. I think Jason Eckhardt's quiet depiction of the New England landscape on the cover of *Fungi from Yuggoth* and many of the internal illustrations represent the real Lovecraft. Very, very few outright horrific images in the book—mostly rooted in New England, some cosmic in nature. Nary a tentacle to be seen. Fergal Fitzpatrick's menacing covers for the Lovecraft variorum editions—if they don't depict any actual scenes from the stories, are quite suggestive of things Lovecraftian, but not overtly. Book covers with squirmy octopus tentacles are not capturing the essence of Lovecraft. It was Steve Mariconda who pointed out that the artwork of Charles Burchfield is quite suited to Lovecraft, and I think you can see that in the cover to *The Ancient Track.*

Q: Did you ever have any desire to write Lovecraftian fiction, or was your response always a scholarly one?

Schultz: When I learned of Lovecraft fandom, it seemed an unspoken requirement that any true fan simply must write a "mythos" story. After all, many of Lovecraft's own friends did, and after his death dozens of fan writers were doing it. As I read some of that work, I realized no one was Lovecraft but Lovecraft. The stories weren't that good even as stories. And every writer felt obliged to invent some new diabolical tome, some new decayed locale, characters whose names seemed to be determined by a roll of three dice with typical Lovecraftian names on them: Tillinghast, Dexter, Pickman, etc. Or like the Business Buzzword Generator. I tired of it. The "posthumous collaborations" with Lovecraft—by a professional writer (and most certainly not by Lovecraft)—were exceedingly poor. "The Shadow out of Space"? Puh-leeze! I won't say there aren't good "mythos" stories out there because I just don't know—I haven't read them, and don't wish to. A writer ought to write what is in him. Pastiche may be a fun game, but I think few have in themselves what Lovecraft did and which he felt called for expression. But I will say that T. E. D. Klein's "Black Man with a Horn" is a remarkable accomplishment. I wrote some crummy poems at first, but realized I wasn't much good at it and abruptly ceased.

Q: Do you have any academic training to actually do literary scholarship? In my experience that begins at the graduate level. Was that the case for you?

Schultz: Absolutely not. I did not attend graduate school, and my career was not academic. And I do not consider myself a scholar. I gather what you have in mind is my work done on Lovecraft's letters, *Fungi from Yuggoth,* the writings of Ambrose Bierce and Clark Ashton Smith, and now Leah Bodine Drake. I do what I do—mostly write endnotes, I suppose—simply by imitating capable scholars. Actual scholars. I think the first genuinely scholarly work I encountered was that of Thomas Ollive Mabbott. A colleague informed me of his famous Poe edition. I got it. I was enthralled! Textual comparisons for derivation of preferred text. History and background of each story and poem. Presentation in chronological order. Annotation to identify literary allusions, historical events, etc. To me, he was the ideal model. And I came across similar work by others. Noel Polk's textual work on William Faulkner, Herschel Parker and others on Melville, Sculley Bradley on Whitman's *Leaves of Grass,* and the whole Mark Twain project.

What possessed me to undertake such work on Lovecraft is beyond me. In fact, I've done very little such work as compared to S. T. Joshi. In the early days, it was very difficult to come by Lovecraft's writings, aside from the fiction. And much travel would be involved to visit repositories with the material needed for consultation. I was thinking that the work Mabbott did on Poe was incredible—consulting early 19th century newspapers, handwritten documents housed in various libraries. Lovecraft, though of the 20th century, would be almost as difficult given the rarity of publications. I was fortunate to have a generous friend in S. T. Joshi, for he sent me copies of many thing that otherwise would have been hard to come by, including his corrected texts—well before they were published by Arkham House.

I'll admit that some of the "scholarly" apparatus in the Lovecraft letters and other works looks impressive. In this day and age it is relatively easy to do Internet searches on all kinds of things. If Lovecraft quotes a passage but doesn't identify its source, Google. books can usually provide the answer. If he refers to a book World-Cat can help to identify it. Most libraries have an "Ask a Librarian" page or link on their website. If I need a copy of something, I can fill out a form, provide a link, and before long have a scan of something I may need emailed to me. Or even just obtain page numbers for bibliographic use (and I have to assume that the librarian consulted actually looked up the desiderate pages, and didn't just make something up). If I were trying to do the work I do now back in the 1950s, it would have been impossible. True, I was younger than 10, but what I mean is that one would have to be a genuine scholar to recognize lines from a poem, to be able to translate Latin or French,

to know much about many subjects. When we encountered lines from verse that needed to be identified, in the days before the Internet, S.T. would gather up an armful of concordances and look through each, trying to identify the passage. Imagine spending hours on a single passage! Now we can identify lines from not just the greats, but the third-rank poets. And my feeling is, if I can find the material, anyone can. Furthermore, scholars read. I search or scan. They're not the same thing.

One other blessing of late. The Library of Amateur Journalism is now in Madison—a scant 70 miles or so from here. It is now incredibly easy to consult the publications that once were so remote.

Q: So, how did you start working with S.T. Joshi?

Schultz: I first encountered S.T. circa 1975 or 1976. I mentioned that I had worked on devising a better chronology for Lovecraft's fiction than that provided in *Dagon.* Joshi independently had the same inclination. He mentioned to Dirk Mosig his dissatisfaction with the published chronology. Dirk, a member of the Necronomicon apa, mentioned my piece to S.T. and gave him my address, and so he wrote me about the matter, and I sent him a copy of my chronology. It wasn't long before S.T. joined both the Necronomicon and EOD apas. Soon thereafter he began working on his Lovecraft bibliography for Kent State University Press. I had been gathering information on Lovecraft's appearances in anthologies. Why such a lame topic? As I mentioned, it was tremendously difficult to find and examine amateur journals and pulp magazines. I circulated a checklist of the anthology appearances in one of the apas and shared my findings with S.T. for the bibliography.

When he was attending Brown (1976–80), I pelted him with queries about various matters Lovecraftian. After all, he was on the ground in Lovecraft country, and himself haunted the John Hay Library for his own work. And so he provided copies of material for my two chief areas of interest—Lovecraft's commonplace book, and *Fungi from Yuggoth.* In addition, he read my drafts of my . . . well, not books, or even articles, on the subject, offering suggestions, and mentioning material I did not know of that bore upon what I had writ-

ten. And so for many years, S.T. was the man to go to. I in no way regarded myself as a peer. I don't even now. He is, after all, the author of a seven-foot bookshelf of reference books on Lovecraft: a bibliography, a biography, "Lovecraft's library," corrected texts of Lovecraft, annotated editions of his fiction, poetry, and essays. My own work would not be possible without all his earlier work.

We first met in 1986, I think. We both had been invited to Steve Mariconda's wedding. Steve had contacted R. Alain Everts about a project he was doing, and Everts referred him to me. As our correspondence grew, I must have mentioned that S.T. lived in New Jersey at the time, same as Steve. And so I believe they had opportunity to meet, and fairly often. At the wedding, S.T. and my wife and I were seated at the reception at the "miscellaneous" table; i.e., not relatives of either family, or local friends. One fellow at the table, struggling to make small talk, asked us how we knew Steve. "We correspond." ??? "We write letters." "Uh, you . . . write . . . *letters.*" I guess that wasn't a good enough reason to be there.

S.T. and I corresponded fairly regularly, I suppose, but as I mentioned, work and family did not allow much time for projects, especially when the children were little. I did manage to stay busy, mostly just researching. August Derleth's papers are at the Wisconsin Historical Society in Madison. Making regular trips there would have been time-consuming. In 1984–86, I had a job that adopted "summer hours." We worked an extra hour each weekday so that Friday we could leave at noon, to get a head start on the weekend. My coworkers would ask, "So what are you going to do?" to take advantage of the free afternoon. "Go to the library." And that's what I did. The UW campus in Milwaukee is an "area research center," and so patrons can have material from other libraries shipped to such a center for use. I had a copy of the register of the Derleth papers in Madison, and used that to order boxes of material. I don't have much interest in Derleth, but his papers contain much information in correspondence with friends of Lovecraft. I gathered an awful lot of good information, but was in no position to make much use of it at the time. I submitted articles to *Lovecraft Studies* from time to time—mostly reviews, I think. And then I started to lose interest a bit.

In 1989, preparations were being made for the Lovecraft centennial the following year. S.T. had suggested me as a panelist, but I was passed over. In protest, he threatened to boycott if I was not on the program. They relented. About that time we undertook our first joint project: *An Epicure in the Terrible.* One thing we thought we might in-

clude in the book was Lovecraft's letters to Henry Kuttner. I typed them, we annotated them. In the end, we did not include them, but instead published them as a booklet. The centennial energized me a bit. When I returned home, and for reasons unknown to me, I started to type Lovecraft's letters to August Derleth. There were a thousand pages of printouts (from a microfilm I obtained from the Historical Society). I typed all that without telling S.T. a thing about it. When I did tell him, when the job was done, he was dumbfounded. But what to do with the things? All I did was input raw text. The letters on the film, and on file, are not in chronological order. That is, dated letters are arranged as best as possible, but undated letters, of which there are very many, are merely gathered at the end of each respective year—someone had roughly dated the letters by year only, but even then many were dated incorrectly by that method. It took many, many years to get the letters into the proper sequence. I'd been annotating the letters all along, but when it came time to try to publish the book, I found that our notation and bibliography style had changed radically—from, say, the Searight or Bloch method to the Wandrei method, by which we loaded as much of the bibliographic work into the back end of the book, so as to have fewer notes. So publication information for a Lovecraft story no

Star Pirate

By - Robert M. Price

longer appeared at the point of first mention in the text as a note; it was relegated to the back. Also, instead of having footnotes, we opted to have endnotes. Among readers, there are advocates for footnotes and for endnotes. We chose the latter because that was the way it was done in Jack London's letters—but then, Jack London wrote very short letters, and the endnotes are very easy to find.

Once the Derleth letters were typed, it became something of a contest to see who could type more letters. I mostly had to be provided with copies to work from, and so I typed Toldridge, Shea, Bloch, Talman, Clark Ashton Smith (such as we had), Strauch, White, and Morse. S.T. typed letters to HPL's aunts, Barlow, Galpin, Price, Rimel, and Long (such as we had). One

problem with the Lovecraft letters was that we could not find any publisher for them. And most—since we wanted to publish them uncut—were far too big an undertaking for our go-to publisher, Necronomicon Press. So we started to find smaller batches of letters to publish there: Searight, Bloch, Loveman/Starrett. We even prepared a few others, but they were not published. One thing we dearly wanted to type was the Arkham House transcripts of Lovecraft's letters. These were the next best thing, though cut, to Lovecraft's manuscripts. (The transcripts were cut down even more to make the final texts for *Selected Letters*.) The library would not copy them—the sheer volume was prohibitive, the brittle pages were side stitched with big staples, and the curator was chary of undoing the archival staples.

So in the early 1990s, S.T. and I made an annual trek to Providence to work on the Lovecraft letters. To consult originals when copies could not be read, and various other tasks. We'd stay for a week or so. About 1997, I was in touch with Peter Ruber. I'd asked him some questions about the August Derleth books he was beginning to publish. He mentioned how he planned to go to Place of Hawks, Derleth's home in Sauk City. I asked if he could keep an eye out for the Arkham House transcripts. We knew there were two sets at least. Wandrei's came to the John Hay Library with Lovecraft's and Wandrei's correspondence and the mss. of Wandrei's novels. The whereabouts of Derleth's set was unknown. It was not among his papers at the Wisconsin Historical Society. Ruber called from Place of Hawks to say he could not find them, only to call back a few minutes later to say he did! He took them with him and doled them out to us over time so that we could transcribe them. If not for the Arkham House transcripts, we would have far fewer Lovecraft letters. So we split them up for typing. I did Kleiner, Morton, and Smith. S.T. did Howard, Woodburn Harris, Renshaw, and Kenneth Sterling. Somewhere along the way, Derrick Hussey approached S.T. to see if he could authenticate a Lovecraft document. Before long, Derrick was part of the typing team, and ultimately the publisher.

S.T. and I grew to partner on more and more projects, though not many of them saw print right away. We had gotten interested in George Sterling, and so I obtained copies of all George Sterling's books and began typing them. S.T. began gathering uncollected and unpublished poetry. As we began collaborating, there were some rough moments. I didn't always turn things around in timely fashion because of familial and employment obligations. And my methods were, I suppose, rather crude. This exasperated S.T. no end, but eventually he got used to my less than rigorous methods, and I improved them as best I could. If I look at our work now, I sometimes can't tell who wrote what. In little matters, like notes, we can mostly speak with one voice.

Another example of this: I had long hoped to gather all Clark Ashton Smith's poetry for publication. I typed much of it, but needed much manuscript material, including his translations of Baudelaire. S.T. was a late comer to that project, but helped immensely in securing material I did not have, and in typing all the translations. We made two trips to Providence in the 2010s, so that we could complete the text. Some transcriptions of poems were full of holes because the transcriber could not read Smith's handwriting. So we pulled out the originals and got to work filling in blanks. We'd pass manuscripts back and forth, asking about possible readings. One might decipher a word or two. The other, upon looking at the slightly augmented text, would offer a possibility to complete filling in the lacunae. It was a means of building momentum, as they say. And so deciphering Smith's handwriting became a tag-team sport.

I remember when S.T. once announced that he wanted (us) to do work on Ambrose Bierce. I said, "Leave me out." I'd seen Ernest J. Hopkins's *Enlarged Devil's Dictionary,* and gotten a pretty good idea of what it would take to research Bierce. Almost as difficult (in my eyes) as Poe. His work was published in 19th century newspapers. How to obtain that stuff? And if possible, probably on microfilm. Well, you know the rest. Together we published eight books of Bierce's writing, and S.T. one more on his own. I did not want to do it, but in time became quite enthusiastic about it. All our work—Lovecraft, Bierce, Smith, Sterling—is detective work. I was less enthusiastic about typing Bierce's writings. Why we did it I'm not sure. Of course, some items turned into books, but we typed virtually all his newspaper writings. Why? The stuff may never be published, though we worked on the *Wasp* era recently before running out of steam, hoping to issue probably six volumes of that. (S.T. currently is working solo on editing three volumes of Bierce's letters.) In the end, typing Bierce's journalism proved very helpful in identifying Bierce's unsigned work in the newspapers, for Bierce gathers some of it into his *Collected Works.* I think I identified at least half a dozen unsigned stories by Bierce. They are unmistakably his. Usually I could find several examples of pet phrasing that he favored all his life in an individual piece, pretty much clinching the fact that he wrote it. By typing all his newspaper work, we were able to identify the first appearances of maybe 95 percent of the poems in

his two collections. The Bierce bibliography is quite an accomplishment, despite a few omissions.

As you know, the partnership still continues. Of a projected twenty-five volumes of Lovecraft's letters, we'll have published I would say 18 by the end of this year. All the others are in the works. Only the Long letters lie dormant, because of lack of access to the actual manuscripts (though we typed the Arkham House transcripts long ago). We have three volumes of Smith correspondence under way—one may be published this year. Because I have some skill at book design, I've formatted many books for S.T., such as three bibliographies for Scarecrow Press. For his own Sarnath Press imprint, I've designed 16 of 40 books of H. L. Mencken's newspaper writings, to say nothing of another dozen books on other subjects. We recently compiled *Ave atque Vale* (in record time). And we're in the final stages of preparing *The Song of the Sun: Collected Writings* of Leah Bodine Drake.

You say I'm a "silent Lovecraftian." Nothing wrong with that, I'd say. Of the various authors mentioned, they are the persons deserving attention—after all, they did all the work. I truly have nothing to say, or very little. Anything I have to say speaks for itself. Of joint projects, if my name appears before that of my co-editor, that means I did most of the work:

typing text, annotating, bibliography, appendices, and the introduction. And so whatever I wrote about Morton, Toldridge, Moe, and Smith is mostly my opinion on the matter, and it ends there. I'm not well-versed enough in broad overviews of Lovecraft, Bierce, et al. to debate such subjects on panels. And I don't think my opinion matters all that much. You'll notice it took almost a decade before there was a piece by me in the *Lovecraft Annual.* I think of myself as a glorified footnoter/endnoter. I mostly write notes. They aren't quite as elegant as haiku, but they have their own compact beauty. If you look at *Commonplace Book, Fungi from Yuggoth,* any of the Lovecraft letters, *The Unabridged Devil's Dictionary* . . . they all are extended annotation riffs. S.T. doubtless thinks differently about his own role doing the same work.

Q: Your experience with S.T. makes me wonder how you found the energy to keep up. Even though (I think) I started research on Lord Dunsany before he did, he still did most of the work on our collaborative bibliography.

Schultz: Well, I have no social life. Haven't been to a cinema since 1980. Therefore, time not spent in the office was spent working on books. For the longest time, such work consisted primarily typing. Lovecraft letters, Smith poetry and letters, Sterling poetry, and 45 years' worth of Bierce's writing. I don't think I kept up with S.T. for many years, but eventually, after the children were gone, I could devote more time to project work. The company I worked for had some very good Word templates for its publications. I observed how they worked, then tore them down to see what made them work. And I learned as many keyboard shortcuts as I could. All this knowledge allows me to work pretty fast and intelligently, and that goes a long way in formatting and editing books.

I think we complement each other in some ways. S.T.'s training gives him better insight into the classics. I tend to see things in Lovecraft's letters that don't always ring a bell with him, and vice versa. For the most part, we can collaborate almost seamlessly on text now, but it took a while to get to that point.

Q: What do you make of the various controversies now swirling around HPL? Is it just a case of the general public belatedly discovering what the scholars knew about in the 1970s? The inevitable consequence of HPL's expanding fame?

Schultz: **Sigh** I don't understand the big fuss. Yes, racism is bad. Yes, Lovecraft was a racist. Guess what? He was a gentleman, a kind man, treated all (I imagine) people well. He encouraged struggling writers and neophytes. He lent books from his library to those who could not obtain them other-wise. He freely gave of his time. He was as generous as his funds allowed. When Helen Sully visited Lovecraft in Providence, she speculated that he was poor, and yet he insisted on paying her way at the boarding house where she stayed. Lovecraft's friend C. M. Eddy was in an even worse way, but Lovecraft did what he could to get him paying work, to feed him, and to clothe his children. The introduction to the book of his letters to Samuel Loveman addresses his supposed anti-Semitism. To say many people of his day were racist does not excuse him from his attitudes. I imagine they were developed during his childhood, at the knee of his grandfather and other family members. Steve Mariconda points out that Lovecraft was a boy at heart, and I imagine nothing would content him but to live as he did as a boy. He doubtless encountered few immigrants or African-Americans in his youth, and their continuing emergence in the Providence of his youth encroached on his New England aesthetic. Many people change their attitudes as they mature. I don't know what to say about Lovecraft. He changed his opinions when he encountered compelling information. Perhaps he would have changed his attitudes on race. Actions speak louder than words, as they say, and what we know of Lovecraft's actions tells me he was a better person than many.

Q: So what are you working on now?

Schultz: The usual. There are still Lovecraft letters to edit. Maybe 7 more volumes to wrap up. And I'm hoping to reissue his commonplace book with some additional information. (Who would have thought that *Xinge* is real?) There are some editions of letters by Clark Ashton Smith nearing completion. But the biggest project—in bulk (760 pages) and importance, I think—is *The Song of the Sun: Collected Writings* of Leah Bodine Drake. Her two published books had only 100 or so poems. This edition will have more than 360 poems, 4 stories, numerous reviews and essays, her letters to August Derleth (and others), a lengthy bibliography, dozens of photographs, not enough information for a biography, but a fair bit of information that no one knows about her, and a refutation of the story that she financed publication of *A Hornbook for Witches* by Arkham House. This was not a project I envisioned, not by a long shot. I heard others planned to do the book, and so in preparation, I started typesetting, awaiting the others to provide more content. Fate or divine Providence deposited virtually the entire project on me. And I continue to do book design for Hippocampus Press and Sarnath Press.

Q: And is there life after or outside of Lovecraft?

Schultz: Man, I hope so. Plenty of books to read, and I want to know my home state a little better. My yoga practice could stand refinement. Once the actual editing of my own book projects ends, I don't foresee taking on any new books. But then, I didn't foresee Drake, either. I don't know that I have the energy to try to assemble Bierce's journalism. Seems to me it would take 50 books to encompass it all. Although much of the text has been typed, it still needs to be proofed and corrected (no annotation). And we didn't quite type *everything.* There's still quite a bit to input from scratch. It is unlikely that a University Press would publish such a work—complete. Fifty books is a lot. Without having to edit Lovecraft letters and the like, it will be easy to simply design books every so often, as long as Hippocampus and Sarnath keep them coming my way—or until I'm fired.

Q: Thanks, David.

END

Another Real—Really Hard— Lovecraft Trivia Quiz

by Steven J. Mariconda

1. In his fiction, Lovecraft's worldview is manifest as an implied desire to:

    a. Foster human needs, interests, and abilities.
    b. Value and respect individuals for their own sake.
    c. Clear off the earth.

2. Lovecraft, as *flaneur* walking the streets of New York City, often was inspired to feel:

    a. A sense of untrammeled & starward *soaring*.
    b. The wonders of revelation & intimation & cosmic identification.
    c. Like punching every god damn bastard in sight.

3. Lovecraft, who enjoyed re-enacting scenes from the theater for company, was outfitted by an appreciative audience of friends with a costume of:
    a. A dark velvet suit with smallclothes and silver buttons.
    b. A periwig, knee-breeches, and three-cornered hat.
    c. A hoop-skirt outfit with bonnet and parasol to match.

4. Reflecting back on his life in the year prior to his death, Lovecraft proudly declared that he had:
    a. Attained perfect knowledge or wisdom by following the teachings of Buddha.
    b. Increased awareness of his inner self and his appreciation of humanity in general.
    c. Laughed aloud on at least four occasions.

5. To assuage a correspondent alarmed by a statement in a prior letter, Lovecraft reassured him: "Do not judge the sort of _____________ I advocate by any form now existing."
    a. Theism
    b. Humantarianism

6. Lovecraft empathised with a severely-depressed correspondent by recounting his own "near-breakdown" of:
    a. 1898.
    b. 1900.
    c. 1906.
    d. 1912.

e.   1919.

f.   1898, 1900, 1906, 1908, 1912, & 1919.

7.   Observing his fellow passengers on the New York City subway, Lovecraft later noted that he felt:

a.   Amused at the spectrum of attire from tuxedos to work clothes.

b.   Amazed at the number of people who could cram into a single car.

c.   Easily able to slaughter a score or two.

8.   In times of stress, Lovecraft managed his anxiety by:

a.   Taking contemplative evening strolls through colonial lanes.

b.   Petting and feeding treats to stray cats in the neighborhood.

c.   Screaming in sheer desperation & pounding the walls & floor in a frenzied clamour to be waked up out of the nightmare of "reality."

9.   While Lovecraft attempted to avoid "irritant & hostile social fabrics," he realized that in life ultimately:

a.   The freedom to develop sincere expression in art is vital.

b.   A healthier adjustment to the environment is indispensable.

c.   A bullet through the brain is the only solution.

10.   According to Lovecraft, "the only things which could ruin life for me" were:

a.   Lack of a sense of purpose and meaning.

b.   Fewer good friends and lack of contact with people.

c.   Hard work and the necessity of living in an unaesthetic neighbourhood.

SOURCES

1. *The Dunwich Horror and Other Stories* (Penguin, 2008), 42.

2. To J. Vernon Shea, 19 Nov. 1931.

3. To the Gallomo, 31 Aug. 1921.

4. To Jonquil Leiber, 29 Nov. 1936.

5. To Robert E. Howard, 27 July 1934.

6. To August W. Derleth, 4 March 1932.

7. To Lillian D. Clarke, 11 Jan. 1926.

8. To Lillian D. Clarke, 8 Aug. 1925.

9. To Lillian D. Clarke, 26 Jan. 1926.

10. To Samuel Loveman, 24 March 1923.

R'lyeh Reviews

Nicole Cushing, *The Sadist's Bible.* **01 Publishing. 140 pp. $7.99. ISBN 978-1945396915. Reviewed by Robert M. Price.**
I often find I cannot review a book without spoiling its surprises, and this is one of them, I'm afraid. So turn back if you've not yet read it and plan to.

I read the first section of *The Sadist's Bible* on Amazon.com. I was both shocked and hooked. It is about two lesbians. One of them, Ellie, has only recently become aware of her orientation toward fellow female flesh— and is married to a fundamentalist minister! Her new friend, Lori, encountered on an internet site, is not married, though she does have a baby son. Ellie is sure she is doomed to hell for her forbidden lust, especially if she acts on it. And if her orientation becomes known her (unhappy) marriage will never survive it. She lives a life of frustration and self-loathing she would like to escape. Lori is frequently sexually abused by her baby's father, to the point she can endure no more. The wom-

en agree to meet up for a Sartrean "final experience" in an out-of-state motel where they plan to indulge in a few days of masochistic depravity issuing in synchronized suicide. Both believe they will immediately arrive in the Christian hell, but that it will be a relief from the pains of the lives they live. This is about the end of the portion I read on Amazon. Obviously, I was sufficiently intrigued to buy and read the rest of the novella.

The story proceeds as both women make ready and embark on their suicide mission. Ellie stops in a motel and a diner, where she chances upon evangelistic leaflets issued by a peculiar sect setting forth a strange gospel of ghastly gloom: God's plan is to degrade creation and everyone in it in order to make them absolutely dependent upon him, in the manner of a sex slave as in *The Story of O*. A deformed angel leads her into the heaven of this God (who is reminiscent of Richard L. Tierney's Lords of Pain who feast upon human misery). But the

God is not a creature of the Cthulhu Mythos, more like the Gnostic Demiurge.

Lori's repeating rapist, the begetter of her radically deformed and defective son, is God. She has played the role of an unwilling Virgin Mary. She, too, is "raptured" by the malevolent deity. Heaven turns out to be a Hell of sexual torture presided over by the Caligula-like Creator. Ellie and Lori are transfigured into creatures like unto the depraved devils depicted in the cartoons of Mahlon Blaine (which festooned the crowded walls of Lin Carter's Manhattan apartment!). Though God had seemingly preempted the two women's date of depravity and death, hijacking them, it turns out he has done them the dubious favor of fulfilling their lusts and hopes beyond their wildest dreams! And nightmares.

I admit my reaction is hardly objective, so what follows is no real judgment, only my reaction. But I found the women's exaltation to transcendent torment to be disappointing. I found the scenario in the earlier portion of the book, set in the real world and poisoning it with nihilism, more horrific and effective than the latter portion, set in an outright fantasy realm, albeit a yucky one. And yet there is profundity in this conclusion. It is a perfect parable of Denis de Rougemont's great study, *Love in the Western World*. That author traced the Western tradition of outlaw love and adultery back through the texts of Courtly Love, through the Medieval Gnostic belief in a transcendent, non-physical love directed to the heavenly Lady Wisdom/Sophia. The ideal was to go above and beyond the "worldly," domestic love of conventional marriage. To pass into an Other world beyond this one. But, De Rougemont argues, the only alternative world of total freedom—is Death. Hence, e.g., popular culture's inexhaustible fascination with vampires, who seem to exemplify this Nightside life—in death. This is what Ellie and Lori sought and were granted by the God of Sadism.

The Color out of Space. **Directed by John Stanley. Starring Nicholas Cage, Tommy Chong, Joely Richardson, Madeleine Arthur, Elliot Knight, et. al. Written by Scarlett Amaris and Richard Stanley. Reviewed by Robert M. Price.**

Obviously this film is an adaptation of Lovecraft's "The Colour out of Space," and of course it takes considerable liberties, as it must. There is a lot of filling in, enhancement of characterization, etc. This is standard fare for Lovecraft movies, right? And for the simple reason that HPL cared not for these elements, his "characters" playing no more role than windows through which the awesome eruption/revelation is conveyed to the reader, over the shoulder, as it were, of Wilmarth, Armitage, etc. So the question becomes: have the adaptors extrapolated in an authentic-seeming manner? Lovecraft's characters are iceberg tips; the movie writers are charged with delineating the shape of the rest of the thing below the surface. In the case of *The Color out of Space* we have the challenges both of updating the characters and of rounding them out. For instance, as to the former, Lovecraft's aged eccentric Ammi Pierce becomes aging hippie Ezra, played by Tommy Chong, type-cast as a drug-addled hippy with New Age beliefs combined with tech know-how. ("Ezra" has been substituted for the equally biblical but less familiar "Ammi.") That's fair. The surveyor, Lovecraft's original narrator, is here named Ward Phillips. He wears a Miskatonic University T-shirt. His role is expanded, making him an employee of the town who tries to warn the mayor about the taint in the water at the site of the projected reservoir. His warnings go unheeded, which explains how the reservoir winds up getting built even though we k now the surveyor knew about the danger.

Now for the rounding out of "flat" characters who are just "phoning it in" in the original. The movie makes Nathan (instead of "Nahum") Gardner and his doomed family into urbanites transplanted from NYC, where Mrs. Gardner worked as a financial advisor, to remote Upstate New York, having relocated to Nathan's inherited farmstead. Nathan has little expertise in agriculture, having repudiated the family business years before, but now sick to death of urban stress. His farming priority is building a stable of alpacas for their milk (inviting the Lovecraftian viewer to make quips about "Abdul Alpaca" and "the High Llama of Leng"). I think it is important to the story for the Gardner family to be innocent rustics suffering from cosmic depredations they cannot have understood much less deserved.

But I will admit that the naiveté is retained in the form of the "Green Acres" cluelessness of the Gardners.

To expand the scope of the action (and the horror) the movie seems to borrow inspiration from flicks like *The Amityville Horror* (the accumulation of disturbing, ominous anomalies) and John Carpenter's *The Thing* (revolting body mutations, melding two or more physical forms, resulting insectoid anatomy, etc.). In HPL's original, the invading radiance is comparatively subtle until the final combustion. In the film, however, it is pretty blinding early on. And though Nathan comments on the color being unidentifiable, you can't really blame the movie for making the eponymous hue a shifting pink-purple. What could they do? (Well, I guess they *could* have made certain scenes sepia tone, negative, or black and white, with the contrasting color eruption.) I couldn't help thinking of Jack Torrance's gradual descent into madness in *The Shining* as Nathan got weirder and weirder in *The Color out of Space*, but Cage's over-the-top portrayals in his other movies make it a bit difficult to tell whether and when he is supposed to be cracking up under the influence of the meteorite.

It occurred to me that we might be seeing hat-tips to both the older "Colour out of Space" movie *Die, Monster Die!* and Michael Shea's sequel novel *The Colour out of Time*. When the alpacas, concealed in the barn, are revealed to have merged into a *Thing*-like snarling hydra, I thought of Nick Adams's reaction to the greenhouse mutants: "It's like a zoo in Hell!" And when Mrs. Gardner starts scampering around on several insectoid legs, I thought of Shea's depiction of the multi-legged embodiment of the color entity.

The Gardner daughter, Lavinia (where have I heard that name before?), is mostly a standard gear in the machine, e.g., urging the others, "Let's get out of here—*now!*" But she is actually quite important. In the very beginning we see her dismounting her horse, clad in a robe, the ends of her hair dyed purple, and commencing a ritual summoning the four archangels of the elements. She prays to them to burn away every trace of her mother's breast cancer, beseeching them to send down a healing but metaphorical fire from heaven. This scene is too complex to be dismissed as a mere throw-away. I have to think Lavinia was unwittingly "calling out of the sky" what turned out to be the alien Color! "Do not call up what ye cannot put down."

And in my favorite moment of the movie, she conjures with the aid of the Avon Books paperback *Necronomicon*! I love it! Here is a very ingenious instance of updating Lovecraft's shuddersome grimoire (which however does not appear in "The Colour out of Space," but who's counting?). The fake, mass-produced Simon *Necronomicon*, not in any sense a secret tome, is nonetheless often these days employed (in vain) by teenage would-be warlocks and witches, who long to be real-life versions of the ridiculous Willow Rosenberg on *Buffy the Vampire Slayer*. (The same nonsense forms the premise of the Harry Potter books/flicks, not to mention *The Craft*: can you imagine the implications if punk kids could really learn sorcery from readily-available books?) The movie takes for granted that you know what bunk it is. But this time—it works!